An Alpha's Grace

Omegas of the New South

Book 3

Sharilyn Skye

Dark Horse Publishing

Morgantown, WV

#CountryRoads

TABLE OF CONTENTS:

QUOTES:

Southern women can say more by the cut of their eyes than a whole debate club's worth of speeches.
~ Allison Glock

Southern women are built on a platform of indelible grace; their capacity to forgive is limitless. But that grace should not be mistaken for weakness because they will light you up for your transgressions, even though they forgive you while they do it.
~ Darrian Battle, The Omega Challenge by Sharilyn Skye

Don't go looking for the reasons
Don't go asking Jesus why
We're not meant to know the answers
They belong to the by and by.
~Chris Stapleton

I told you that we could fly
'Cause we all have wings
But some of us don't know why.
~ INXS

CHAPTER 1

GRACE

Some stories can't be told by any but the persons who lived them. Who better to get inside my head than me? I never dreamed that one day I would find so much happiness. All those years lived in a cage did not allow me to think that the sun could shine so brightly upon my life or that I would learn the song of an Omega.

I didn't even know that's what I was. How could I? My whole life had been lived behind bars. If I was ever a child, I don't remember. If I had ever been free, I don't remember that either. Parents? No clue. The only thing I understood was a small cell with a pile of dirty blankets for a bed.

And I knew men. And pain. I'd never seen the sun, moon, or stars that I remembered, but I knew starvation and cold. Animals know more about life than I did before I was freed.

The saddest part to me now is how normal it all seemed then. You learn what you live, and if you live in darkness, that is all you expect. You can't know a flower exists if you have never seen it bloom.

Then my world exploded in a burst of flames and sound as Eve Justice Hatfield flew into my life in a streak of red hair and brazen attitude. She opened my cage and set me free. She killed the people who had held me prisoner and tortured me for all the

1

years of my life. Their blood painted the walls before fire purged the place of all sin.

A woman did that.

Frozen in fear and shock, I struggled to leave my cage, but I did, and saw the sun for the first time. I felt the warmth upon my naked skin and smelled the sweet air of freedom, only I was more frightened than I had ever been as a caged thing. What was freedom to those who have never known it? Terrifying.

It's terrifying.

I could understand only a few words, couldn't read or write, and could barely speak. My age was a mystery. I was certainly older than Eve, but no one knew for sure. Doctors examined me in those first hectic days and would only say I was between twenty-five and thirty-five. I felt ancient.

Mirrors terrified me. What an odd fear that is. I knew I had short, ragged black hair and solemn gray eyes. I remember my keepers often shaving my head to keep lice from infesting my cell. In the months I'd been free, the hair on my head grew, and no one offered to shave it again. It was a wild, dark mass that scared me when I saw it on my pillow.

Once freed, I didn't sleep in the dark for a long time.

Eve and the other Omegas taught me what they could about the dynamics and the world beyond a six-by-six cell in the depths of a basement. Someone came daily to make me shower and eat. They talked to me and read me books. I was given food to eat that upset my stomach because it contained nutrients I was not used to.

I learned about taste.

And learned I loved hot things. Spicy things. I'd been frozen my entire life, and so I also loved hot water, hot blankets, and hot sauce the moment I was exposed to them.

Try as I might, I could not say thank you.

I don't think I've ever thanked them.

When Eve and Lorelei came to me, explained what was happening, and told me I was leaving my room, I went. My heart sank, and what little bit of peace I had found fled, but I left anyway. Doing as they asked was the only way I could think to repay their kindness. And even if that meant leaving safety, I would do it.

I know they thought I was broken and unfixable. They told me it was a last-ditch effort to save my life. The truth is, I couldn't understand what they were talking about. Not then. I didn't feel broken. I felt perfectly fine. Only time could show how broken I really was.

Yes, I had to be reminded to eat and shower. Yes, I had to be told to brush my teeth and go to bed. I always forgot to brush my hair or go to the bathroom. At the time, I was caught up in the fact that there was a difference between night and day. I was so struck by the sight of the sun or a bird that daily life activities were beyond me. I couldn't function under the weight of my freedom. A plant that never flowers doesn't know it can until it does.

I followed them out into the bright fall sun that led to a fate I didn't understand. Leaves the color of the explosion that freed me dotted the trees and courtyard, overwhelming my senses. Their rich smell crashed into my nose, sending me into a tailspin, and I froze.

Unable to take another step, they waited patiently as I adjusted to the noise and sensory overload of the outside world. Birds singing pulled my attention to a large tree with fire-red leaves in the brick pathway's center. My eyes skipped along the branches, trying to find the bird singing that particular song; then they landed on a man.

He stood straight and tall, his hands clasped in front of his body. I dropped my eyes and couldn't look up. Wooden steps carried me forward, and the cell door slammed shut again.

CHAPTER 2

DARRIAN

I watched her attention flit over the tree above my head and couldn't take my eyes off her. With every hesitant step she took across the courtyard, she paused, eyes darting right and left. I'd seen rabbits do this as they crossed a newly cut hayfield. With the protection of the tall grass gone, they doubt every step forward.

That was Grace.

Her nostrils flared, and her eyes widened as her feet made the dry leaves beneath them crinkle. Her ragged hair was black as black can be, and the sunlight made it look almost purple. It blew in the wind in every which way as if encouraging her to bolt.

She was a tiny thing. Absent were the curves Omegas boasted; she looked a bit like a child. I hadn't seen her until that moment and hoped I hadn't made a mistake. She was frighteningly frail.

Broken is not just a term for a thing's physical state; it can also refer to a mental attribute. In Grace's case, it was possibly both. It was like I could see the jagged pieces of her. They were jumbled into a semblance of a person, but the person was not there in its entirety. It was heartbreaking.

No one knew her past. Grace herself rarely spoke and had to be taught the few words she occasionally said. She'd been used for one thing and nothing more. She'd hadn't known how to clean herself until the other Omegas showed her. Even still, she had to be told to do so. If The Alpha and the New South's marines hadn't already wiped out the compound where Grace had been kept, I would go there myself and do it on principle.

Unable to take my eyes from her, I watched as her steel-gray eyes found me and dropped to the ground before they could take me in. The hairs on her head vibrated with the strength of her tremble. But she didn't run. Even though I'm not sure she would if she thought to, that's what the absence of free will would mean for her.

Lorelei and Eve waited patiently as Grace stared at her feet. They'd said they would explain and give her a choice. They had also said that Grace didn't understand free will, so I wonder if that is true. The girls had wanted to put Grace down like a rabid animal, and I couldn't understand or allow that to happen. Very few broken things cannot be fixed.

Grace moved her feet again, never looking up. With each step toward me, she grew impossibly smaller, and I wondered if I was wrong. By the time she was within arm's reach of me, she had curled around herself so tightly that she was half my size.

"Don't forget what I said, Darrian," Eve warned. "Friend or not- brother-in-law or not, I will end you," Eve growled, putting a protective hand over her pregnant belly.

Eve meant it. I'd been warned before this day of all the various and painful ways I would die if I hurt Grace in any way, but had agreed to her demands and even understood them. I also knew that she would kill me in a heartbeat if she felt I reneged on our agreement.

A few short weeks ago, Lorelei had been attacked by three Alphas who felt they had a claim to her. None of those Alphas were alive today. Lorelei had admittedly killed two of them. The other was shot dead after being convicted and sentenced for rape by the high court. His sentence had been comparatively light for the crimes he committed, but he never left the courthouse grounds.

The shooter hadn't been found, but Eve was a damn good shot with a bow. And so was Lorelei. These Omegas were something different, and I know well enough not to fuck with them.

Over the last few weeks, the girls had been a near constant in my life. They frequented my parents' farm and never failed to shoot, stab, or drag home something for ma's freezer. They were wild, dangerous, and unpredictable. I don't know how my baby brother and The Alpha dealt with them, but I'd also never seen those men happier. The situation was intriguing.

I'd never even considered courting an Omega until I met Lorelei. I'd been happy enough with Meghan, my former alpha girlfriend. I'd known she cheated; I'd known she would never be faithful. Alpha females are wired differently. Their drive to procreate is so strong that they would sleep with any male that moved until they conceived, which in itself is rare. I understood that. Alpha males are driven to bond, but females are not.

What I hadn't known was how much money she had embezzled from my investment firm. Lorelei had found millions stolen from me, and Eve was going after my ex to get the money back. And these were Omegas. I hadn't known an Omega could be so fierce, independent, or intelligent, if I am honest.

It had almost been a joke when I asked them if there were any quiet, less fierce Omegas I might court, but then they had mentioned Grace. Then they mentioned putting her down.

And that's how I came to be standing here waiting for the most frightened creature I had ever seen to make her way to me. Lorelei and Eve were careful not to touch her as they flanked her, taking up positions on either side of me. I'd been in the Marines. I knew what it looked like to walk a prisoner to their death. By all intents, that's how the scene played out.

"I understand, Eve," I said, reverting from calling her EJ, as I had recently come to do. I looked Grace over as she stood in front of me, trying to make herself small enough to disappear.

Her skin was sallow, and it was hard to tell what it would look like if she were healthy, which she was not. Dark circles shadowed her eyes and carried down to her cheeks. Her face was sharp-angled and heart-shaped. Her pixie-like chin dipped to her chest, and thick lips formed a flat line while long black lashes shielded her eyes.

Her coloration was odd in the New South but not at all unusual for an Appalachian woman, or so I'm told. The Omegas from the Seventh District had brought diverse and exotic beauty to the capital, spreading it like fall leaves through the town. Healthy, Grace's beauty would be striking.

"Grace, this is Darrian, the Alpha we told you about," Lorelei said, her voice soft and without the sharp edges she could use to cut a man in half.

"My new Master," Grace whispered, her voice serrated from disuse.

"No, sweetie. He is not your Master. You are to help him with household duties, and in return, he'll care for you in the Alpha way. We talked about this, remember?" Lorelei used her voice like magic, and the girl in front of me drooped.

"Was I bad?" Grace asked, piecing the words together slowly. She trembled harder, and I felt like complete shit because I had caused this.

"This isn't punishment, Gracie. We're your friends, and we care for you. We want to help you," Eve added, reaching a hand to tuck Grace's hair behind her ear. I watched Grace's eyes fall closed at the touch.

"Broken?" Grace asked.

"Use a complete sentence, Grace," Eve softly admonished.

"You are giving me away because I am broken?" she asked, the words tumbling together like she wasn't sure they were correct.

"You're not broken, Grace. But you need something to do and time to get better. Darrian is a good Alpha; he'll help you, and I will kill him if he harms a hair on your head. But you need something more than an empty room to help you heal," Eve finished.

But she'd said the wrong thing, and I watched as the tiny woman in front of me shook so hard it looked like a seizure. Her eyes flashed up at me, wide and terrified. Eve's words had been a trigger, and Grace's screams echoed off the walls of the Capitol building. She fell to her knees, clutching her head and pulling at her hair until it came out in clumps.

Eve's hand flew to her mouth, and she dropped to her knees next to the wounded woman at our feet. I shooed her away and scooped Grace up. She was mine now. I'd known from the second her tentative steps bore her to me that there was no going back.

My mother was right when she said I was good with broken things. She'd been there the night I talked Eve and Lorelei into giving me a chance to save Grace's life. She'd told them that if anyone could do it, I could. I believed that. As I held the shaking woman close to my chest, I had to believe it.

Where a group of Omegas failed, I could not. Grace had been harmed through no choice of her own, and her life shouldn't be forfeit because of that. I purred for her, and the thrashing and screams stopped because instinct is just that. Instinct. It's irresistible.

Grace went limp in my arms, eyes rolling into her head as her brain short-circuited and did the only thing it could. Grace shut down. Only the even rise and fall of her chest gave away that she hadn't simply died from terror.

"Before you think to threaten me again, Eve Jennings. Remember, I'm trying to save her life when you both thought to end it," I said, walking away with the limp Omega in my arms.

"I'll send her things," Lorelei offered.

"Don't bother; there's nothing left for her here," I added over my shoulder, not slowing my steps.

I had taken a private shuttlecraft to Greenville, leaving my transport at the airhub in Atlanta. The shuttle waited at The Alpha's helipad, and in a few brief minutes, Grace was buckled in, and we were gone.

After nuclear warheads went racing from continent to continent, high altitude flight became impossible. But the nation was small and international trips were no longer necessary. The thirty-minute flight passed quickly. Grace opened her gray eyes slowly as the shuttlecraft descended into Atlanta. I watched them open and snap closed when she realized where she was and who she was with.

She sat bolt upright, her hands in her lap. She refused to look at me after her quick assessment of the scene, choosing instead to stare at the floor.

"Grace, my name is Darrian, and that is what I want you to call me," I started. Grace didn't move or look at me. "I have some rules that I need you to understand and do your best to follow," I paused, thinking about what my mom had said on the ComLink.

She'd reminded me that structure was integral to the healing process for the damaged horses we sometimes found. They felt safer when given a clear set of rules. She'd tried giving them immediate freedom, but it hadn't worked, and they'd become more fearful, not less.

"First, when I speak to you, you must look at my face. Second, you will answer what questions you can as best you can. And third, you'll tell me if I do something that scares you so that I stop doing it. Do you understand? I don't intend to harm you," I said while Grace continued looking down, refusing to raise her face.

"Grace?"

"Yes, Master," she mumbled, digging her nails into the skin of her hands, causing half-moons of blood to rise.

"Don't call me master, Grace. I want to be your friend. Call me Darrian, and I have rules, too. I will not harm you, Grace. And I will always strive to be honest with you." I reached over and undid her seatbelt slowly to present no threat. "I won't hurt you," I said when she pulled away. "And I would appreciate it if you didn't hurt yourself." I gave her hands a pointed look, and she relaxed her fingers, wiping the drops of blood on her clothes.

"Darrian," she said, trying my name out. It sounded unsure on her lips. Her accent was unlike the other Omegas. It was deeper, even deeper than my own or my parents'.

The thing about accents is that you tend not to notice ones like yours. Grace's was unlike any I'd heard before. We didn't know how she came to be in the compound in the Seventh District, Elkins. Jameson said the place was wild and that she could have come from any of the hollows or mountaintops in the area. Or none. Without her telling us, it would likely remain a secret.

The doors of the shuttlecraft opened with a swoosh of air, startling Grace. Her head whipped around, and she made a small cry. I walked calmly forward, expecting her to follow.

"Why are you doing this? There's nothing left to take," she said, her voice halting and hoarse. "They took it all." She never raised her head, already breaking the rules.

"Grace, I won't take anything from you, but you may surprise yourself and find there's something to give." I looked behind me, seeing if she'd follow.

Shoulders slumped, she did. I drove a newer post-war Ford and had left it in the airhub's parking lot. It's not that new vehicles weren't made; they were. They were just expensive and harder to come by. The New South also imported goods from other countries, exporting some as well. Trade was slow-moving as it had to be done by boat, but it happened.

Goods were even imported from the New North and Middle West. Although they were trusted less than those across the ocean. The war had changed everything for everyone. Things still functioned, but on a smaller scale than before.

Once the states had been united, but that bond was broken by political infighting and strife. It was irrevocably shattered when the bombs fell, and brother turned upon brother.

I often wondered what the days before the war were like and how good it might feel to cross a vast country on wide-open interstates. So much had changed, and I wondered if they thought it was worth it when the dust settled. The Blue and The Gray; The Red and The Blue, had it really mattered?

Pausing at the passenger door, I opened it for Grace, who gave me a long look before slipping into the seat. The bright Atlanta sun reflected off her dark hair as she sat, curling her tiny frame around herself. With a sigh, I walked around the car, hoping once again that I hadn't made the biggest mistake of my life.

The drive to the condo was short, but Paces Ferry was crowded with people shopping at the pop-up bazaar that, well, popped up most weekends. I wove my way through the crush of people, glad that the windows in the car were tinted deeply enough not to allow anyone to see in. Grace shrank lower in her seat, if that was possible, as people moved out of our way.

Cutting across Peachtree, I finally turned into The Graydon and home. Grace went rigid as the twenty-two-story building loomed closer. A slight tremble started in her hands, and I stopped the car before entering the parking area that led to my elevator. "What is it, Grace?" I asked, turning to her.

Her eyes were wide when they snapped to mine and immediately dropped.

"Grace, I am asking you a question and expect an answer," I said firmly. Her trembling stopped. A leader must be strong, but also understanding.

"A cage," she stuttered, briefly looking my way so as not to break rule number one.

I started to admonish her, but stopped, looking at my luxury condos with fresh eyes because I suppose it looked like one. The tall, white building was one of the tallest left in Atlanta. Most of the others had been leveled. The Graydon had stood but sustained massive damage; it had only reopened ten years ago.

The People of The New South had fought to rebuild this area. It had been destroyed in two Civil Wars, and they did not take kindly to that. It took years to gather the materials to make The Graydon livable. Once finished, it was prime real estate again. It kind of looked like a cage, though.

"Grace," I said. "It's not a cage, but I agree it looks a little like one. See the very top floor there?" I asked, pointing my finger skyward. "That's our home. The penthouse belongs to me."

"It's too high!" she said, covering her mouth with her hand quickly. "I'm sorry, Master." She cowered, breaking my heart.

God, I'd made a mistake.

"I'm not your master, Grace." Driving under the cement canopy, I shifted the car into drive and eased into the gated parking area. The temperature dropped as the bright southern sun was blocked.

I had a designated spot and an elevator that went straight to the top floor. The penthouse had cost me a fortune, but had been worth it. I liked the privacy it afforded and could walk to the firm if needed.

I placed the car into park and turned to look as Grace's panicked eyes roamed her surroundings.

"It will be okay, Grace. Let me show you."

CHAPTER 3

GRACE

The man called Darrian walked around the nose of his car, giving me a moment alone to catch my breath. Except when I inhaled deeply, it just forced more of his natural scent into my lungs. As my only experiences with smells weren't good, Darrian's scent was unrecognizable to me. Nothing about him smelled bad. I eventually learned that he smelled of fresh air and pine trees, but it would be months before I realized it.

He opened my door, stepping back to give me space. I darted by him as quickly as possible. Acting like he didn't notice, he led the way to a small steel box with one button. Small spaces were cages, and cages were bad. I'd lived in one for all the life that I remembered.

I'd had bars for walls, with a toilet and small sink in the corner in open view of the larger space beyond. I'd had to climb to get to the outside world, letting me know I'd been underground. Looking at the colossal white building as we approached brought terror to my heart.

I shook as the doors to the steel box closed, and it lifted smoothly into the air. Crying out, I sank to the floor of the thing, covering my face with my knees. Darrian stood calmly, saying nothing. Then it was over, and the doors opened again. Sunlight streamed into the tight space, urging me out. Darrian held the

17

doors open as I peeled myself off the floor and scuttled into the room on my hands and knees.

I stepped into a house the likes of which I'd never seen. Done in white and stainless steel, it was the epitome of what I came to know as sleek, modern design. Gray and white throw rugs covered concrete floors polished to a smooth shine. Art hung on the walls, illuminated by discrete lighting, and I wondered at the cost.

I hadn't understood money or the value of things until Eve and Lorelei explained it. They'd tried to take me shopping, but the act of leaving my living quarters was terrifying, and I couldn't get further than the lobby of the Capitol building where I'd lived.

Instead, they showed me pictures on a computer screen and how to pay for items with a coin card The Alpha supplied. I only used it once and never again. The entire ordeal was uncomfortable.

I'd enjoyed the peace and relative safety my room had given me. It was small, but large is overwhelming when you are used to a cell.

Overwhelming was the penthouse's first name. Open sightlines were everywhere. We stepped into a grand foyer, and I could see from the formal great room all the way into the kitchen. To my left and right were massive terraces that wrapped around the exterior. There was nothing but windows, and being surrounded by air was about the last thing I could handle today. I sat down on the floor and rocked myself from side to side.

But then I was scooped up and placed gently on a soft white couch. "On the furniture, Grace," Darrian said gently.

I unclenched my eyes and watched him move through the space, take off his suit jacket, and remove cufflinks. He was comfortable in the vast, empty room. I was not.

Groaning, I slipped back to the floor. "I'm falling." The words came out before I could stop them, and I worried I had spoken too freely. I wasn't used to being allowed to share my thoughts.

"Very good, Grace." He paused his smooth movements, looking at where I sat on the floor and giving me a wide smile. "This building survived The War, albeit barely. I promise you will not fall."

He ignored me as he pulled food from the stove and placed it on the counter. The smell floating through the air was fantastic, and I wondered what it was.

"I had Helen leave supper. She made Indian food. Eve said you liked spicy things; I hope she didn't exaggerate."

I watched as he loosened his tie and ran his hands through his hair, and down his face. Sighing, I scooted on my knees to him and unbuckled his belt.

"What are you doing, Grace?" he asked, stilling my hands. His voice went hard, and the look on his face was no longer pleasant.

I hung my head, unsure what to say. He pulled me to my feet and gripped my chin in one hand, bringing my face to his. "I asked a question, and it is one that you can answer."

"You're angry. When men are angry, they want," I stopped, forcing the next words past my lips, "something." I finished, unable to say the words.

In my experience, men wanted to fuck when they were angry. Or happy. Or anything. I had no experience with men that didn't involve my body, and I was out of my depth.

"If you ever suck my cock, it will be because that is your desire, not mine. Do you understand?" Darrian asked.

"No," I answered simply, shying away in anticipation of the strike I knew would follow. It never came.

"I didn't bring you here to serve me, Grace. I brought you here so you could see how things should be. Please don't offer yourself from your knees again. I won't accept. Whatever experiences you had, they are in the past." Letting go of my face, he walked to the stove.

I sank into a chair at the table. Eve and Lorelei insisted I learn to eat at a table, but it was awkward and uncomfortable. It didn't feel natural to sit upright while eating, and sometimes I dropped food.

Darrian slid one plate onto the table, sitting in front of it. "Come here, Grace," he said, sliding the chair back and opening his arms to me.

My eyes rounded with fear, and my gaze darted left and right because maybe I had misunderstood what he said.

"Grace," he said again, watching me expectantly.

Lowering my eyes, I moved and stood in front of him. Scooping me off my feet like a doll, he settled me onto his lap.

"This is Rista," he said, picking up a fork and putting it near my mouth. "Take a bite."

I froze, stiff on his lap. He made a soft noise in his chest, and my back went limp. He'd made the same noise earlier, but I thought perhaps I'd imagined it. Lorelei had mentioned an Alpha's purr, and I thought maybe that's what this was.

Opening my mouth, I wrapped my lips around the fork carefully, trying his food. An explosion of taste blew through my mind, and I groaned low. Behind me, Darrian chuckled quietly, shifting so that the hard planes of his chest supported my spine.

"This," he continued when my deep moans stopped. "Is vindaloo." He held the fork to my lips again. The scent of the spicy sauce had my nose running, but I took the bite offered. Again, the groan came, and I had no hope of stopping it.

Darrian fed me as my nose ran, and my body groaned at the pleasure of all the spicy dishes. He added naan and chicken curry to the fork; before I knew it, the plate was empty, but he hadn't eaten a bite. He set me aside and rose to refill it. A tall bottle of chilled water sat on the table, and I took it, pouring myself a glass. I drank it and poured another.

Darrian returned to the table and pulled me back into his lap. He offered more, but I was so full I was uncomfortable. The soft noise in his chest continued even as he ate. It was confusing to sit on a man's lap and have them feed you. I didn't understand, but didn't hate it, if I'm honest.

I sipped water and sat, swinging my feet while he finished. Darrian was so large that his chairs were taller than a standard chair, and my feet didn't reach the ground.

"Try the tea," he said, pulling a small, delicate cup toward me. It was a soft, cream-colored cup with a silver lip; inside, a light brown liquid steamed. I brought the cup to my nose and inhaled the light floral scent. "It's chamomile; it won't keep you awake."

I didn't know what tea was or that it could keep you awake. Picking up the cup, I fumbled it in my hands. Darrian caught it expertly before it could fall and break, but some of the tea spilled, and I started to cry.

"Hush, Grace, it's okay. It's just tea. Most of it is still there. Try it," he said, not angry at all. Judging by the look of everything around me, the cup was worth far more than I was.

My tears turned to sobs, and I scurried off Darrian's lap and onto the floor behind the couch.

The scrape of his chair warned me he was coming, but when his tall frame folded to meet mine on the floor, I almost fainted.

"Grace, look at me," he demanded, his voice silky and smooth.

Forcing my eyes up, I blinked once and dropped them again because I couldn't. I just couldn't.

"Everything is okay, Grace. You can stay here for a few minutes, but I expect you back at the table once you compose yourself. Understand?" The noise in his chest never stopped, and already I felt calmer.

"Okay, Darrian," I choked out.

He went to the table, and I heard him settle into his chair. I took deep breaths, scrubbed my hands on the hem of my long skirt, and followed. Standing silently at the edge of the table, I waited. He slid back, opened his arms wide, and I climbed onto his lap.

"Good girl," he said, sipping from the refilled cup of tea. He offered it to me, and I took a sip.

It wasn't spicy, but it was sweet. It tasted like fresh flowers smelled, and I liked it. I found the warmth soothing when it hit my belly and sipped the tea as Darrian finished his supper. Pushing away from the table, he shifted me across his hips and rose.

"Let me show you around," he said. His voice resonated, but his accent kept it from sounding harsh, and instead of scaring me, it soothed me.

"I can walk," I offered.

He stopped, turning his attention down to me. "Am I hurting you?" he asked, shifting me in his arms so that I could see his face.

I thought about his question.

"No," I answered.

"Am I making you uncomfortable?" he asked again.

"I just. I can walk," I said, avoiding the question.

"I know you can, but it pleases me to carry you unless you are uncomfortable with it." He shifted me back and walked toward the great room.

"Is this an Alpha and Omega thing?" I asked, unsure of the answer. Eve and Lorelei had tried teaching me about the dynamics, but it was a confusing topic. I didn't feel like an Omega. I felt like nothing.

His steps faltered. "Yes, I suppose it is," he answered. "Through the gallery this way are two bedrooms and a den. The den is where I spend most of my time when I'm home," he said, walking into a smaller room holding more comfortable furniture. A fireplace burned cheerfully, and the setting sun glowed yellow, orange, and red on the horizon. One entire wall of the room was windows, and a wide sliding door led to a terrace outside. Furniture was scattered on the massive balcony, and I wondered if he knew enough people to fill it.

The thought was frightening.

"Through that door is the guest wing terrace, although I use it myself sometimes. My family visits, and when they do, I need every bit of the square footage," he laughed. "One-third of the over eight thousand square feet of this condo is outdoor space, and you can make use of it any way you like." He turned, heading away from the cozy den and back into the hallway that he referred to as a gallery.

Why would I use that much space, let alone outdoor space? I knew of no activities requiring so much room. I said nothing as Darrian continued the tour.

We passed more carefully placed artwork along the walls, beautiful, dreamy pieces with soft colors and pastoral views placed so expertly they seemed haphazard. I'd seen nothing like them, but that wasn't saying much.

"This is our wing of the house," he said as he carried me back across the great room and down another gallery. We passed a small bathroom with only a toilet and a sink, and I shivered when I looked in. At least it had a door.

At the end of another art-filled hallway, we passed through a large sliding door that looked like it belonged outside. Shifting me, he flipped a switch, bathing the gigantic bedroom in warm light.

"This is our room," he said, sliding me off his hips and letting my feet touch the floor. "Through there is our bathroom. This is my closet," he said, sliding open another of those strange barn doors. "And this is yours," he added, pushing open another.

The closet he called mine was larger than all the rooms and cages I'd lived in put together. Clothes of every color and variety hung, and a cushioned bench seat stood in the middle of the room, as if one would simply go into their closet and have a rest. I didn't know what to say.

Racks of shoes went along one wall, and the floor was lined with baskets of bedding. A door in the back opened to the bathroom, and I wandered around, touching everything.

The bathroom was bigger than the closet, and far too bright. A massive, glass-walled shower with no door stood at one end, while a square tub large enough for a swim filled the other. Not that I could swim.

The floor was warm beneath my feet and made of a silver-veined, shiny rock. Silver reflective tiles accented the white and gray walls, and my breath was sufficiently taken.

Darrian walked into the room, laying a fluffy white robe across the side of the tub. "I won't bathe you tonight. Someday, I hope you'll let me because it would please me," he said, stepping out of my personal space to turn the knobs on the bath.

Steam rose, and I sighed just looking at it. I'd never had a bath, only showers. I watched as the tub filled. Everything was so foreign that I was on the verge of a breakdown. Darrian's chest rumbled through it all, and I wondered if making that noise hurt.

"Take a bath, Grace. I'll leave you alone." He turned, leaving the bathroom through the door to his closet, shutting it softly behind him. I felt his absence when he was gone.

Stripping my clothes, I ran my hands over the hard lines of my body. White scars ran over my skin, and my bones stuck out everywhere. Eve and Lorelei fed me, but I never gained an ounce. I hadn't been hungry in months, but my body refused to use the food it was given. If anything, I'd lost weight.

The Omegas didn't understand it, and neither did I. It just was. I thought I was probably dying, only I wasn't sure from what. I slipped into the steaming water with a loud sigh.

Simple pleasures were something I hadn't understood until I'd had a warm, spicy meal followed by a hotter shower. I hadn't known how nice it was to sit on a toilet behind a closed door or wear warm clothes. My old room in the capital had air conditioning and a window I could see out. These simple pleasures were taken for granted by everyone around me, but I enjoyed every single one of them.

I let the water come to my neck before turning it off, and I soaked for a long time. I didn't know what Darrian wanted, but figured I would find out soon enough. So far, he'd fed, clothed, and bathed me, and that wasn't bad. Whatever else he might want was a small price to pay for using this bathtub.

He'd fed me with his hands and carried me on his hips. It should've been weird, but wasn't. Maybe I was an Omega, after all. I slid to the edge of the tub, picked up bottles of shampoo and conditioner, and smelled them before choosing one that smelled a little like Darrian and washing.

CHAPTER 4

DARRIAN

The sound of her loud sigh and the soft splash of water went straight through me. God, this sucked. My cock was so hard that if I didn't relieve myself, it might break. I walked to the back of the house, into a guest bath, and jacked off into a toilet. Gripping my knot to keep it from expanding, I finished in about forty seconds. Grace was getting to me. This was another instinct and couldn't be helped.

I'd known this would be hard as hell, but my control was ironclad, so I didn't worry. Feeling better, I was back in my bedroom before the smell of my shampoo and body wash carried to me on the rising steam. I groaned.

I'd set about teaching Grace about the Alpha and Omega relationship through demonstration. Yes, sex was a part of that, but there were other parts just as important. Something so simple as her smelling like me could be a trigger. I needed to care for her, and she needed to feel cared for. She needed to learn that she was the center of that bond, not me.

I hadn't approached this in words because I knew she would be terrified if she knew where I was going. Instead, I showed her how it should have been for her from the beginning. Eventually, I hoped the rest would come.

The concerning part was that she didn't look, smell, or react like an Omega. Testing proved she was, but that was the only indicator of her dynamic. With time and care, I hoped she would find herself.

I turned on the gas fireplace and opened the sliding glass door to the cooling Atlanta night. After pouring a glass of whiskey and changing into more comfortable clothes, I made my way to the terrace and stood at the rail, watching the Atlanta skyline light as the sun finished setting.

I lit the gas firepit, too, and eased onto the loveseat facing the flames. I heard Grace rummaging in her closet and hoped she was okay without help.

Lorelei and Eve told me she had no will. No independence. No self-determination. They said she needed to be told to do everything. I hoped she would be all right doing the simple task of dressing, but didn't want to take it for granted.

Her head poked out the closet door, looking left and right quickly. When she spotted me, she walked forward, clutching the edges of the robe together.

"Do you need something, Grace?" I asked her, sipping my whiskey as I watched her vacillate between asking me and not.

"What do you want me to wear?" she asked, dropping her eyes.

"Look up, Grace. Don't forget," I said, reminding her of my rules. "What do you want to wear?"

"I," she started, but stopped immediately. Her face scrunched up, and her gray eyes faltered. "I like dresses better than jeans. The jeans are tight on my legs."

The jeans weren't tight on her legs per se; they were constricting, maybe. Eve said she'd been naked when they found her and that she had a hard time wearing any clothing- almost like she never had. I wished for the millionth time that I could go back and kill those bastards.

I rose from the outdoor sofa, walked across the terrace, and headed to her closet. "There are drawers of nightgowns for you. It's been a long day; maybe dress for bed." I opened the drawer in the closet and pulled out a soft, yellow nightgown. It would look beautiful with her black hair and gray eyes. She clutched the gown to her chest, waiting for me to leave before shutting the door. I refilled my glass, waiting for her to come into the room.

The first thing I saw was how the soft yellow gown skated her lean legs, falling to the floor. It did indeed make her look beautiful. I mentally slapped myself for suggesting it. Grace carried a laundry basket of nesting material in her arms, shocking me. She sniffed the top layer, then dumped it on the floor in a heap and crawled on top.

Maybe she was an Omega.

It wasn't a nest, but it kind of was.

"What are you doing, Grace?" I asked, humor bleeding into my voice.

"Going to bed," she answered, barely looking up at me through her lashes.

"Grace, we don't sleep on the floor. Neither of us. You will sleep on the bed."

"With you?" she squeaked, her voice rising an octave. She glanced out the open door to the terrace, and I thought she might jump, but I was more than proud of her for voicing her thoughts.

"You are my Omega. You will sleep on the bed with me," I admonished softly.

"Yes, Master." She rose to her feet, leaving the nesting material in the corner.

"Grace."

"Yes, Darrian," she said, supplanting one word for the other, but the tone was the same. Defeated. Tired. Empty.

Maybe I should let her sleep alone, but I didn't think so. The goal was to show her what the Alpha-Omega relationship looked like. It was to show her that not only was she safe with me, but she would also thrive with me. She needed to understand that all the horrible things that happened to her were not natural, but the things we shared were.

I would take it slowly and push nothing onto her, but I wouldn't back away when things became uncomfortable.

"You're safe, Grace. Come to bed," I added, moving to close the dark gray curtains against the Atlanta night.

Trembling, she walked to the bed, one slow step at a time, and ignored the way her eyes stared at her feet as she came.

"Do you want my clothes off?" she asked, her voice low.

"I want you to be comfortable," I answered, praying that didn't involve her sleeping naked. I might control myself, but that would test my will early on.

Her eyes went back to the pile of blankets in the corner, and I knew she would be more comfortable there, but I had given her my expectation that she sleep beside me. I watched as her small hand pulled the blankets back, and she slid in between them. Turning onto her side as quickly as she could, she rolled away from me.

I flipped off the lights and slid under the sheets beside her, careful to keep my distance, and laid still until I heard her soft intakes of breath and knew she was asleep.

I'd gone into this with a plan. As an investment manager, I excelled at long-term strategies. I could play the long game better than anyone I knew, and had prepared for this to be a long road with many losses and gains along the way. What I hadn't planned for was how much it would matter to me if I failed.

Until I met her, it'd been easy to say I would give Grace back to Eve if I couldn't help her. Now, I knew better, and my cold and somewhat calculated approach to 'fixing' Grace fell apart.

Omegas bring out the Alpha's desire to protect when they bond with them. I hadn't even considered claiming her, but my instincts were screaming at me to care for her. Fix her. Destroy her enemies. Every fiber in my being demanded that I take her body and soul. Grace wasn't much of an Omega right now. My God, what would it be like when she was?

It's a wonder my brother hadn't killed me when I raced to his mate like a water buffalo. I'd been a fool. I'd thought Jameson was an out of control idiot for his displays of possessiveness and protectiveness of Lorelei.

Turns out I might have been wrong.

I had no bond with Grace, but I felt my hair stand on end when I thought about her situation.

And I'd known her for a day.

When I was sure she was asleep, I leaned on one arm and looked at her face. It was at that moment that I knew I was in trouble and that I'd made a mistake. The lean lines of her body lay rigid against intrusion. Dark eyelashes fell across her cheek, and the need to protect her was so strong. I knew I could never let her go. If this project went down in flames, I was going with it.

CHAPTER 5

GRACE

I woke up in the still of the night. The room was dark, and no light filtered through the curtains, even though the city beyond was brightly lit.

Darrian lay on his back, arms across his chest. His face was relaxed in sleep, and as my eyes adjusted, I could make out his features. His skin had a reddish tint to it, and a few freckles dotted his nose. His lips were full, but the lower one ridiculously so, and his dark hair was tousled in sleep instead of perfectly combed, which made him look less fierce.

And Darrian looks fierce.

The men from my compound never looked like he did, and they were in control of everything, or so they thought. He sighed, the suddenness of it almost sending me rushing off the bed. He hadn't hurt me. Not once had he threatened me. He'd given me rules that weren't hard to follow in theory.

I rose, walking to the bathroom. I hadn't eaten so much in my life. Something about sitting on a man's lap and being fed made me starved for more. I'd never had an appetite, but with Darrian's hand on the fork, that changed.

I'd never been taken care of, and I'll admit, it wasn't horrible. It didn't hurt or chafe. I didn't cry because of it. It almost felt...nice.

I emptied my bladder and cast a longing look at the pile of blankets in the corner. The bed wasn't uncomfortable, but it was smooth and even, forcing my body into a straight line. I liked the uneven sprawl of a pile of blankets as it was easier to shift and adjust myself. I hadn't used the bed in my old room in the capital. For as long as I could remember, I'd slept on floors.

I climbed into the bed anyway, edging just a tad closer to Darrian. The condo's temperature had dropped drastically as the night cooled, and Darrian was like a furnace. The warmth he put out eased my stiff joints and warmed my skin.

One of the worst things about my cell had been how cold it got at night. Even in the summer, the temperatures dropped wildly. Add that the compound was deep in what Eve called the West Virginia mountains, and the cold was multiplied tenfold. I slid as close to Darrian as I could without touching him to soak up some of the warmth of his body.

I woke up alone, sprawled out in the center of Darrian's enormous bed, which I burrowed into. Under the blankets, I'd made a little hole for myself. I was warm and comfortable, unwilling to move, but starving.

The smell of bacon and maple drifted in the air, making my stomach growl. I peeked out from under the covers, and once I saw I was alone, I slipped into the bathroom before I could be caught. After refreshing myself for the day and applying deodorant and cream the way Lorelei showed me, I went to the closet.

Rows and rows of pants, shirts, skirts, and dresses filled my vision. There wasn't a color in existence that wasn't represented, and the sheer magnitude of clothing was overwhelming. I stood for several minutes before pulling out a long, gray dress that would allow me to blend into the background of this place.

I tiptoed on bare feet down the gallery, looking at each piece of art. What manner of man afforded this place? I didn't know. One look around, and I knew there was more furniture than I'd seen in my entire life.

Gripping the wall, I peered around the corner, trying to find where Darrian was and if I was safe. A glance showed he was sitting at the table, sipping from a cup and reading on his tablet.

I ducked behind the wall when he called to me. "Grace, come and eat." He didn't look up, and I froze a moment before pulling myself around the corner, using the wall to hold me up.

"Good morning," he said, looking expectantly at me.

I remembered this. Eve had taught me about manners and being polite, even when you don't feel like it. As I'd seen her knock around more than one person, I wasn't sure she'd learned her lessons, but I tried anyway.

"Good," I started, looking over his shoulder at the woman in his kitchen before continuing. "Good morning," I finished, cocking my head at her. I wondered if she was his wife. She was a fair bit older than he, but she was beautiful. Her skin was ebony, and her smooth black hair was pulled into a bun. She bustled around the kitchen, offering him one thing or another. The smiles she gave were fond.

Most of the men in the compound had wives, but they still came to my cell. Women came too. I wasn't sure what it meant, but none of it was good. Not for me.

Seeing my suspicious gaze, Darrian said, "Grace, this is Helen. Helen helps me while I'm at work; I often work late, and without her, I'd be a mess. She's going to show you a few things you can do while I'm gone during the day." He put his tablet down and watched me carefully.

"I'm an old, bonded Omega, dear. Nothing to fear," the woman said as she gave me a kind smile that showed no teeth.

The Omegas had taught me about the dynamics and how they usually interacted with one another. I'd been around plenty of people in my life, and most of them hadn't been harmless, regardless of their dynamic. Maybe she meant something else.

Confused, I walked forward to where Darrian beckoned. "Please sit," he said, sliding out to make room for me.

Wordlessly, I slipped into place on his lap.

"Coffee?" he asked, offering me a cup filled with dark, hot liquid.

I lifted the cup to my nose and inhaled the sharp, rich scent. I took a sip.

"It's very good," I said, and it was. I didn't remember having anything like it before.

Helen brought a plate and set it in front of Darrian, who picked up a fork and offered me a bite.

"Have you had pancakes?" he asked.

"Yes, I like them," I answered.

"These are better; Miss Helen makes the best pancakes in the New South. Don't tell my mom I said that," he added with a chuckle and a wink at Helen. "Bacon?"

I took the bacon from him and shoved it into my mouth whole. I loved bacon. "You should eat," I said around the bite.

"I will when you're taken care of," he said, offering me another bite of pancakes.

"You don't need to waste time feeding me," I said, snatching the bite from the fork and practically mantling over the food.

"It makes me happy to feed you. You're my Omega, and this is part of what that means. I need to care for you. It's a desire I can't quell," Darrian said, bringing another bite to my lips.

Helen smiled at us again; her eyes twinkled in the light as she watched, and I thought the whole situation bizarre.

Bite by bite, he fed me until the plate was empty. Then Helen refilled his plate and placed a thick, white drink in front of me. "It's a smoothie," she said. "We'll have you right as rain in no time."

"I'm not sure I can; I'm stuffed, Miss Helen," I said, running my hand over my rounded belly.

"Give it a shot, dear," she said kindly.

I didn't trust her. In my experience, people who were kind to you wanted something. If I were honest, I didn't trust either of them. The nicest visitors to my cage were always the worst.

None of the Omegas had been overly kind once I'd been freed. They'd been direct, they'd been informative, and they'd been perfunctory, but they hadn't coddled, and I appreciated it. There's far more honesty in those things than in kindness.

Even Darrian hadn't shown me overt kindness, making me trust him a little more. He'd cared for me, but he was firm in the way he cared. I sniffed the smoothie warily.

"Go on, dear. It'll put some meat on your bones. It's my grandma's recipe," she smiled again before grabbing Darrian's empty plate and refilling it.

Darrian purred softly behind her; the vibration of his chest was so soothing that I relaxed against him. Picking up the smoothie, he brought the straw to my lips. "Give it a try," he said.

I leaned forward, intending to take a small sip, but once the smoothie hit my tongue, my brain exploded with a new feeling. Leaning forward, I gripped the glass to my chest, guarding it and drinking it down.

Since my rescue, I'd gone crazy over *taste*. How something so simple could be so amazing, I don't know, but it was. That first smoothie was divine. Vanilla, cinnamon, and a hint of sweetness mixed with a thick base of cream or yogurt, and I couldn't stop myself from drinking it in seconds. There wasn't time to savor; I had to have it. Right now.

With a sigh, I finished the smoothie, then promptly and embarrassingly fell asleep on Darrian's chest. In the back of my mind, I heard his soft chuckle and low purr. His movements were slow as he turned the pages of whatever he read on his tablet or brought to his lips. I felt so warm and my eyes wouldn't open, so they didn't.

Eventually, he rose, carrying me down the hallway to his room. "I have to leave for a few hours, but when I return, I want to take you outside for a short while. Rest up," he whispered, settling me back into the bed and covering me with heavy blankets.

The doors closed, and his footsteps echoed down the long hall. Oddly, I missed his warmth and snuggled deeper into the mattress to imitate it.

I awoke hours later, judging by the way the light had shifted in the room. I rose with a stretch, feeling relaxed and peaceful. It was odd for me, and I thought maybe I'd been drugged. It happened before, but I didn't feel sluggish. In fact, I felt quite good.

I smoothed my wrinkled clothes before tiptoeing into the hallway, the floor warm beneath my bare feet. The fireplace in the great room cast soft shadows on white walls. The air smelled fresh and clean, with no trace of Helen or Darrian. I walked the length of the room to the elevator entrance, where I found it unlocked.

I could leave.

But go where?

So far, all Darrian had done was feed me. Would that change? I couldn't say because I'd never been fed before. There'd only been enough food shoved through the bars of my cage to keep me alive, nothing more.

I'd had dirty blankets and a toilet in the corner.

I'd been dragged out of the cage nightly or trapped in the corner and fucked roughly more times than I could count. And I lay there and let them do what they wanted because that's all I could do.

And I remember nothing other than that life. Nothing. My earliest memories were the same. Surely there was something before. Right? I wasn't born in a cage, unless I was. My knowledge of the world was minute.

So why would I leave? Where would I go? The door to this cage was open, so I convinced myself I hadn't traded one for another. And maybe I hadn't. My surroundings were luxurious by any standard, my belly full, and body clean. There was nothing to complain about.

I walked to the kitchen, noticing how every surface shone. No fingerprints marred the steel surfaces, and the reflective silver tiles glowed in the dimmed overhead light. I went to the refrigerator, hesitant to touch it.

"Grace?" Darrian said from the foyer, making me jump from the door.

Gripping my hands in front of me to still their shaking, I answered. "In here."

"I'm so sorry for being late. There's been a lot of fallout from Meghan's theft and fraud. All of my meetings went long." He rounded the corner, catching me near the oversized refrigerator.

"I'm sorry, I wasn't going to touch it. I swear," I whimpered, scuttling away from him and dropping on all fours to make myself small, but he caught me.

"Grace," he admonished. "This is your home. You are allowed in any room, any cabinet, and most certainly in the refrigerator. You are my Omega. What's mine is yours. All of it," he said, taking me by the hand. "Come here." He pulled me forward, placing my trembling hand on the door handle. "Open it."

I cut my eyes at him, watching his face. He was smiling slightly, and his face relaxed and open. He didn't appear angry. It could've been a setup, but it didn't seem that way.

"Open it," he said again, this time more firmly.

I opened the door.

The inside of the fridge was packed full of every kind of food you could imagine. Bottles of hot sauce lined one shelf, bringing a smile to my lips. I grabbed one, opened the cap, and put it to my lips, sucking down the wonderful liquid.

Behind me, Darrian burst into laughter, "You're ignoring the plate with your name on it, Grace."

I capped the bottle and looked. On the shelf at my eye level was a plate with a card that said 'Grace.' I couldn't read, but I recognized my name. The others had tried to help me, and I knew a word or two. "Oh," I said, replacing the hot sauce and taking the plate. I looked around for a microwave.

Darrian plucked the plate from my hands. "I'll get this; you grab a bottle of water."

I watched as he put the plate in the microwave and pressed the buttons before taking a tall bottle of water and shutting the door.

He took my plate to the table, set it down, and pulled me onto his lap when I got close enough. "How was your nap?" he asked, bringing a bite of tender, rare beef to my lips.

"Good," I answered, swallowing without chewing.

"Grace," he admonished. "Complete sentences and chew your food, please," he finished, bringing another bite of food to my lips.

"My nap was good, thank you," I said, waiting to take the bite until I was done speaking.

I'd spent my first few days of freedom eating. Eating with my fingers from bowls or plates. I didn't care where the food came from; I ate it. The other Omegas took turns teaching me to use silverware and to have basic manners. I tried to remember those lessons now as Darrian offered me another bite of food.

"After lunch, I'd like to take you into town to pick a few things. I also planned to get your hair trimmed," he said, offering me buttered potatoes on a fork.

I froze, "My hair?"

"Is beautiful, Grace, but you deserve a touch-up. All women go to the salon, I believe.

"I see," I said, taking a bite of potatoes so I wouldn't have to say anything else.

"I mean it, Grace. You're beautiful. Getting your hair done is something women do and enjoy. I want you to have that." He put another bite of beef to my lips, and I wished he'd just give me the fork already so I could eat as fast as I wanted. The food was good.

Finally, the plate was empty. I grabbed the water and emptied the bottle in long drafts. Darrian watched me suspiciously.

"Grace?" he asked.

I stared at him in response, waiting for the rest. I could tell by his face that I would not like it.

"When was your last heat suppressant shot?" he asked carefully, looking at me like I was a bomb that might go off. He sniffed the air discreetly.

"I'm sure they gave it to me before I left, I suppose. I'm fine if that's what you're asking," I answered, feeling my cheeks flame red.

"Yes, I want to make sure that you're okay, but I also don't want to be unprepared if your estrous should come."

"It won't," I answered, rising from his lap, feeling self-conscious.

"You sound sure," he said, watching me move away from him.

"I am," I said as firmly as I could manage. Darrian was getting into dangerous territory. There were so many things I was afraid to talk about, and this was one of them.

"How?" he asked, taking the plate to the dishwasher.

"I've never had one," I answered with the only truth I knew.

The plate dropped from his hands, shattering on the floor.

Startled, I backed to the wall.

I didn't know what an Omega was until Eve and Lorelei told me, and I still didn't believe them. I'd never had an estrous that I remembered. Not one. The Alpha authorized the suppressant for me, but I didn't think I needed it.

I was broken. I might not be what they wanted.

Maybe that's how I came to be in a cage in a basement in the middle of hell. Perhaps whatever family I'd had rejected me because I wasn't normal. Darrian was going to a lot of trouble for nothing, and now he knew.

The Omegas assured me I was okay. They'd had a doctor run tests, and she'd found nothing wrong, but I think having an estrous is something one remembers. All my genetics came read Omega; there was no explanation, none other than mine. Something was very wrong with me, and it had always been.

"You can give me back if you want, Sir," I said, reverting to formalities.

"Fuck. Grace, no. You're fine. I'm just surprised. I'm actually glad that isn't something we need to worry about right now. It's a relief. An Alpha's response to an Omega in estrous is not always…appropriate," he said, fighting to suppress a smile.

"I see," I answered, unsure of what he meant.

"My brother. God, my brother, and Lorelei. They are living proof that the road to hell is paved with the best intentions. Come on, let's get you out of here and into the sunshine before it's gone." Darrian moved past me, ignoring the fact that I had plastered myself to the wall. "Ready?" he asked.

"Yes," I answered, knowing it was a lie.

CHAPTER 6

DARRIAN

When Grace said she'd never had an estrous, I almost lost it. How can that be? Lukas said her test results came back normal and that she was physically healthy. What the fuck had happened to her psychologically that had shut her body down? God, I hoped I never found out. It broke my heart that she must remember every detail. I'd never asked, and she'd never offered. A better man would've pressed her to talk.

I was so far over my head that it would be laughable if her life wasn't at stake. I pasted a bright smile on my face and pressed the down button on the elevator, sending Grace into a panic; she seemed to hate them.

Grace was one of the most beautiful women I'd ever seen, but her captors did a number on her. Her hair had been chopped or shaved unevenly, and it grew at all angles. Her nails were chipped and sharpened to razors in places, often drawing blood when she clenched her fists.

She had no idea how to care for herself beyond the basics, and I thought a trip to the salon was in order. I'd hand-picked the place after asking around, hoping to find the perfect someone. I prayed I picked right.

When the elevator stopped, Grace peeled herself off the wall and walked to the car. I ignored some of her less concerning behaviors, thinking that, with time, she would adjust, because if I made a big deal of every little thing she did, she might shut down. Whereas if I showed her that elevators were just a normal part of life, hopefully, she would come to agree.

I opened the door to the car for her, shutting it when she slid onto the cool leather seats. We left The Graydon and headed onto the crowded city streets toward the heart of Atlanta.

I'd asked around, getting the name of an old Omega who'd done hair out of her apartment before NS304. Now that she could, Clara had opened a salon in an upscale neighborhood, using her dynamic and her history to make a fortune.

Turns out, Clara had been through more Alphas than was decent in the South. Her mates kept dying, and somehow, she'd survived them all. She'd done a spread for Peachtree Magazine, showing off her shoulders and their myriad claiming marks. No one knew how she did it, but I had my suspicions.

Why was I taking my naïve, damaged Omega to see a scandalous, possibly murderous one? Because Clara understood. She would understand Grace and possibly help her. If nothing else, there'd be no judgment from the old lady. I'd met with her this morning and knew that she was the perfect person within minutes.

Grace craned her neck, checking out everything we passed. Her hands were glued to the side of the car, and her back was turned to me. She hadn't been out of our condo since she arrived, nor out of the Capitol building since her rescue, and it was time. Life moved on whether or not we wanted it to.

I slid her window down to let in the warm fall afternoon air. I caught her smile in the side-view mirror, and it was worth every penny this trip would cost.

The breeze blew her shaggy black hair around, and her eyes closed as the sun warmed her face. The penthouse was surrounded by windows, getting constant sun from either side, but there's nothing like it on your face.

I cruised side streets, letting her get a feel for Atlanta's flavor. The Old Girl survived two wars and had come back from the brink of death so many times, and that seasoned the air around the once great city. As more and more people came to her, Atlanta grew and changed again. She was a survivor.

Like Grace.

When we finally pulled into the parking lot at the salon, Grace had settled. She'd leaned back into the soft leather seats, closing her eyes. She was so pale from being underground that her cheeks were already pink from exposure.

Grace waited while I walked to open her door. I don't know whether she was simply unsure what to do or enjoyed the act. Both thoughts made me smile. I was surrounding her with people that I thought would help, and together, we would get her through this.

"Oh! My dear!" Clara exclaimed when we walked through the door. "That skin! Those eyes! We'll fix the rest. You're simply marvelous!" The older Omega glided to Grace, grasping her smooth hand in a weathered one. Clara's southern accent was deeper than even my mother's, if such a thing is possible.

I watched a befuddled look cross Grace's face, fading almost instantly. She glanced my way and, seeing my smile, offered a small one of her own.

"Darrian told me you were beautiful, but he did not do you justice. That coloration, I declare, you're stunning."

"Thank you, ma'am," Grace whispered, looking like a trapped bird with her hands in Clara's.

"Don't ma'am me, sugar; call me Miss Clara. Where'd you get those gray eyes, honey?"

"I can't be sure," Grace answered, wilting just a little. "It's an Appalachian thing, I'm told."

"Well, never you mind about it, let's sit that big Alpha of yours down, and we'll get you right as rain in no time," Clara said, giving me a pointed look.

I sat.

I shifted so I could keep Grace in my line of sight. It was uncomfortable not to keep my eyes on her. Despite everything, she was still an unbonded Omega, and the world remained dangerous.

"What do you want me to do with your hair, sugar?" Clara asked after placing Grace in a chair before a large mirror.

"I," she paused, catching my eyes in the mirror.

"I don't know. What do people do to their hair? Wash it?" Grace said, shrinking in her chair.

And Clara laughed, and the sound filled the shop until every head turned. Initially, Grace looked mortified, but after a moment, she smiled, too. And then she laughed. Never had there been a more beautiful sound.

And I knew I'd been right to bring her.

Her laughter eased a worry I hadn't known I held. Grace was going to be okay.

Me? Well, I couldn't say the same. I was twisted up over this sweet, unsure, brave, and beautiful Omega. For better or worse, there was no going back for either of us.

"Just don't shave it, please, Miss Clara," Grace said, silencing the surrounding shop. "I don't care for that style," she finished, not noticing the way Clara's hand stilled in her hair or how she glanced my way.

I'd warned her, but even the direst warnings often go unheeded. I watched her smile slip for a moment, grateful that Grace was oblivious.

"I don't like that style on a woman either," Clara said, recovering quickly. "Now on a man? My lands, on a man, I'll take it." She gave Grace a wink and resumed the slow perusal of her hair. "Come now, let's get you started. I have a plan," she finished.

And what a plan Clara had. I watched in wonder as she painted the strands of Grace's hair and placed them in tinfoil. All the while, Clara whispered to Grace, making her laugh. Sometimes those laughs were at my expense, but I didn't care. The way Grace looked at me and smiled made whatever nonsense Clara said worth it.

When the painting of Grace's hair was finished, Clara led her to a small table, taking her hands and clucking over them.

"My lands, sugar," she hummed. "Soak these here a spell." She dunked Grace's hands in a milky substance, then rose to grab polish from the wall.

Then, one by one, she cleaned and shaped her nails before painting them a soft pink. Grace's eyes rolled back more than once at the feeling of her hands being cared for. It was incredible to watch. Sad, but incredible.

As they were closer to me, I was more aware of their conversation, even as I gave the illusion of privacy by pretending to read a magazine.

"You're going to look so good for your Alpha, dear," Clara advised, her tone serious. "Darrian is a catch, and he couldn't care less if you wore a potato sack and got a perm, but he's going to be crazier about you than ever. Such a beautiful girl," she whispered, concentrating on Grace's nails. "You know, Darrian is Atlanta's most eligible bachelor. Maybe even the New South's now that The Alpha is mated. Not only is he all the talk, but he's also sweet and gentle. It's clear as day he's smitten with you."

"Smitten?" Grace asked, not understanding the word.

"He likes you, dear. I think he likes you quite a bit," Clara said with finality.

Grace looked confused, whispering, "I don't think that's possible, Miss Clara. I'm broken; they've all said it; I've heard them. Even if he likes me, he won't when he realizes I can't be fixed. Maybe my hair can, but not the rest."

"Now, you listen here, young lady," Clara started, her tone making me want to get up and end this conversation, but I forced myself to wait.

"Darrian isn't like other people. I know darn well that boy never said you were broken. And here's something you need to understand. Scars are a roadmap of where you've been, not where you're going. You hear me? Maybe you have scars, and I can see the pain you've lived in your eyes, but that's behind you.

"You take your future, and you grab it, and you wrestle that mean bitch into submission, you hear me, girl? Tomorrow belongs to you. Scarred and scared are two different things, and it's okay to be both. You get me? It's okay. But you gotta let'em go." She gave Grace a fierce look, and so much of her own past shone in Clara's eyes, and Grace saw every bit.

I turned the page of the magazine, having no clue what was in it. My body relaxed into the seat, and I felt faint. That old, murderous Omega was right, and I prayed Grace knew that.

"Time to shine, sugar!" Clara declared, giving Grace a long look. Then, she took Grace to the sink and pulled the foils off.

I could hear Grace's soft groan when the old woman massaged shampoo into her scalp, and it gutted me.

It didn't matter that Grace didn't smell like an Omega or do anything personally to trigger that instinct in me; I am a man first and an Alpha second. That moan made my cock twitch, and I had to force myself to think about anything else to calm it. I took two long showers a day, but that might not be enough, I sighed.

As bad as she was, Meghan had taught me a lot. Dating an Alpha female is daunting for an Alpha male. Most days, I felt like I'd been run across a cheese grater. Only rarely did she make me feel like what I was. Sex was on her terms, never mine; it was raucous, tending toward violent. I had a lot of practice denying myself, and that practice would come in handy.

Maybe Grace wasn't the only damaged one.

I looked up, catching her eye in the mirror. While I was lost in my thoughts, Clara had taken scissors to Grace's hair and was now blowing it dry with a big, rounded brush. Somehow, Clara had taken Grace's black hair and made it darker. It shone almost blue-black under the salon's bright lights. How do you give the night sky dimension? Ask Clara. I did not know, but she did it.

Unable to stop myself, I stood, arms limp at my side. I watched as she turned the dryer off and smoothed Grace's hair around her face. The tips of the front brushed her collarbone; the rest was stacked a bit, making the overall appearance even. Clara had removed the jagged layers, taking none of the length, and it was stunning. Grace was stunning. My mouth dropped open.

"That's how a man should always look at a woman, Grace. Alpha, Omega, or Beta, if you find a man that looks at you like that, keep him," Clara whispered to Grace, turning her toward me.

Grace looked up at me from beneath darkened lashes. During this process, Clara had put just a touch of color on her face. Her lips were stained a shade darker than was natural, and her long lashes swept her eyebrows when she blinked. It was going to be a long night.

"Grace, you look stunning. You take my breath."

"Thank you," she replied after a long pause. She tucked her hair behind her ears, and the gesture made her look so young. No one knew her age, not even Grace herself, but that simple move made me think the doctor was mistaken and that Grace was years younger than proposed.

"Are you ready for supper?" I asked. "I arranged something special for you." Had I known how affected I would be by her makeover, I would've skipped it, though. My nature was screaming at me to take her home and away from prying eyes.

"You don't need to do that; just anything is fine," she said, avoiding my eyes.

"Just anything is not fine. Not for you. This is your city now; I want you to see its beauty. You've been cooped up far too long; it's time to live," I said, calling her to me with an outstretched hand. She came to my side, and we stepped into the Atlanta night.

We walked. It wasn't far. I'd reserved a table at my favorite steakhouse, Bones. It was original to the old Atlanta and had reopened some twenty years ago. The food was fantastic, and their menu varied.

The Maitre'D opened the door for us, and the smell of food made my stomach growl. Grace inhaled sharply, her eyes closing in pleasure. "Mr. Battle, your table awaits," the man said, guiding us through the crowded room to the back, where a warm fire burned.

Everyone Grace passed stared; she didn't notice, but I did. There wasn't a woman in the room more beautiful, and they knew it, even if she didn't.

"Thank you, Mason," I said when we'd reached our table. "I'll get it." I pulled Grace's chair out for her, watching as she sat at my invitation. As Eve and Lorelei suggested, Grace never thought to question; she simply did as I asked. And perhaps that wasn't right. Did she understand any of it, or did she just go along?

I took the seat across from her, not bothering to look at the menu. "We'll have the 2186 Chateau Minuty," I said when the waiter came. "And the seared tuna for starters." I thanked the man, and he left.

I placed my napkin in my lap, watching Grace mimic my motions.

"This seems like a nice place, Darrian," Grace said, using my name. It startled me so much that I looked her way. Her eyes were a little round, but she appeared calm as she sipped water and looked around the room.

"Your presence makes it that much nicer," I said, meaning it.

She laughed, shocking herself. "I feel like a different person. The hair, the makeup, everything; I don't feel like myself," she said, looking unsure.

"What do you feel like?" I asked.

"Cinderella," she said, dropping her eyes.

"Say again?" I asked, confused.

"The Omegas had me watch it. They said that it was an introduction to the Alpha-Omega relationship," she answered, her voice cracking at the end.

"You're right," I said, seeing the stunned expression bloom on her face. "It is a decent introduction," I hurried, not wanting her to second-guess herself. "But you look like a queen, not a princess," I added, accepting the cork from the waiter, smelling the wine, and inhaling its floral notes.

I poured Grace a glass and handed it to her. "Do you like it?" I asked as the waiter stood nearby. She took the glass as if it might explode in her hand, sniffing it. A smile spread across my face at her reaction because she was a natural at this. She took a tiny sip.

"It's terrific," she said, setting the glass down.

"Excellent," I said. "She'll have the twelve-ounce filet medium rare with grit fritters, bacon mac, and asparagus. I'll have the mixed grill with corn pudding and collards," I ordered.

"Excellent choices, sir." The waiter walked away, sliding through the crowd.

"I hope you don't mind that I ordered for you," I said, taking a bite of tuna and cutting it up on a plate I slid to her.

"Of course not, I wouldn't know where to start," she said with a sigh. "I'm just grateful not to be in your lap in front of all these people," she said, biting her lip.

"Some actions are for private moments, Grace. You are your own person. My drive to care for you can be tempered when need be," I said, giving her a wry smile. "You're welcome to disagree with me, Grace, anytime. I'm not asking you to disagree with me constantly, but you can do that as well," I amended as she smiled.

"I wouldn't think so," she said. "Is there anything you've done that I should disagree with?" she asked. Her face was open, and the question genuine. She really didn't know.

"I don't think so. Not yet, anyway, but the day will come. Always tell me if you don't like or want something, and I'll try to listen." I cut a few more small bites of the delicious tuna and passed them to her.

"You'll try?"

"The best I can, Grace."

"Well, thanks for not lying to me and promising more than you can give. I'll try to do the same." She sipped her wine, looking like she'd been born in a five-star restaurant.

Our arrival hadn't gone unnoticed. Clara was right; I was talked about. As Atlanta's most high-profile bachelor, others paid attention. I hated it. But that's just how it went in the South. I knew that there would be a mention of our dinner in tomorrow's society papers.

"Why are you doing this?" she asked, meeting my eyes.

It stunned me to silence because she worked hard to avoid looking at me.

"I wanted to, Grace."

"You wanted to try to fix a broken Omega?" she asked, her voice shaking.

"You're not broken. Your wings may be damaged, but you're no less an angel," I said, taking her hands in mine. "I've worked hard my whole life, and have more than most ever will. I want to share that to give back to the world that has given me so much.

"I've been in investments a long time, and I know a good one when I see it. Grace, I asked for you. When Eve told me about you, something clicked. I'm not just fancy dinners and sound investments. I've made mistakes, but I felt like maybe I had more to offer than money and status. There have been bad investments, wrong people who left me damaged too. Maybe together we can be something bigger than the pieces we hang on to," I finished.

She scrunched her nose, trying to understand. Her eyebrows grew closer together, and I could tell she was thinking. "I've told you I have nothing left to take, Darrian. Maybe your idea isn't bad, but I don't know how to do what you're doing."

"And you don't need to. Let me do the giving, and you do the taking. It makes me happy. Does it make you unhappy?" I asked, sliding the rest of the appetizer to her.

"No, I guess not, and I don't think I'm unhappy. I'm not sure what I feel, if anything at all."

"Then let me teach you."

Our meal came. I took her plate, cut her steak into bite-sized pieces, and passed it to her. It took everything I had not to scoop her into my lap and feed her, but I wanted to show her that life wasn't all one thing, and that surely it was better than what she'd lived before.

She hummed appreciatively as she ate, making it impossible for me to keep my eyes off her. I offered her pieces from my plate as well, enjoying the sounds she made with each different bite. In the end, she ate all of her plate and half of mine, and it made the night more than worth it.

CHAPTER 7

GRACE

I'd never been more confused in my entire life. The only thing I understood since my rescue from The Seventh is that abuse is easier than kindness and far less intimidating. Darrian was losing weight. I could see it in the way his suit fit.

He focused so much on feeding me that he was starving himself. Still, he pushed his food my way, and I ate it. I liked his meal better than mine. It was filled with spices, and the lamb burst with flavor. And the pheasant sausage? Who knew such a thing existed? Incredible.

Darrian had been so kind and gentle, but I waited for the other shoe to drop. Indeed, it hung over my head like an anvil.

"Grace?" he asked, tilting his head in concern. "Are you okay?" The dim light caught the freckles spattered across his nose, making me notice them.

"I'm fine, thanks," I said, taking a big breath and looking away. "I'm...uncomfortable with the fact that you let me eat all your food," I said, looking away immediately so I couldn't see the anger on his face.

"Grace," he said, his voice low. "Look at me when you speak," he added.

I looked up, fearful of what I might see. The last thing I expected, honestly, was to see him smile.

"Thanks for your concern; I appreciate it more than you know," he said. "It's the first time you've voiced your opinion without me asking," he said, reaching for the hand I forced myself not to pull away. "It pleases me to see you well fed, but I'll eat more myself, since it bothers you. And to that effect," he said, nodding to the waiter who seemed to hover just at the edge of things. "We'll take the mountain high pie and two cups of coffee," he added with a smile. "Charge my card with a thirty percent tip, and we'll see ourselves out when we're ready," he finished, dismissing the waiter completely.

"As you wish, Mr. Battle; it's been a pleasure to serve you as always," the man said, walking away with a smile. My knowledge of math was rudimentary, but thirty percent of a lot is a lot. I imagine the waiter was pleased to serve our table.

It gave me an idea. "Do you think I could do this?" I asked, making my voice as loud as it would go, noting it still came out as a whisper.

Darrian's wine glass stilled on the way to his lips. "Do what, Grace?" he asked, placing the glass down.

"This job?" I said, my voice sounding weak, even to me.

"You could, of course. Do you want to?" Darrian asked, his voice changing. I didn't understand the context of the change, but I understood that it was a change.

I thought about it. These waiters were everything I wasn't. How could I even talk to people when everything terrified me? "I guess not," I sighed, slumping in my seat.

"I had hoped that you'd learn from Helen and help me around the house. She wants a reason to spend less time with me, I think," he laughed. "But if you're interested in something else, you can come to the firm and see if you'd like to do something there."

"You want me to be your housekeeper?" I asked, thinking I might be able to manage that.

"No. I want you to be my wife, Grace. Someday I hope you want that too." He looked me dead in the eye, and I flinched, nearly dropping my wine. "I will not lie to you, Grace. If you ask me a question, I'll always answer to the best of my ability."

"Your wife?" I stuttered, panicking at the word. I'd known many a wife; they were brutal things. They'd beat me when they found their husbands on me, then sneak back once the man had gone.

The wives touched me, put their mouths on me, or fucked me with objects; to what end, I never knew. They just did. The wives were always far more dangerous than the husbands. The only thing I had to worry about with a husband was a cock in one of my holes. Some of them even talked to me, but the wives? No. Never.

"I…" I started, unable to finish.

"Grace, look at me," Darrian started. "You're white as a sheet. Explain what I've said to scare you." He reached for me, and I gave him my hand. It looked like he was ready to pull me across the table and onto his lap, and I could hear his soft purr and see his concern.

I took a big breath, feeling it shudder out of me. "Wives are dangerous," I tried, hating that the hand he held shook. "They...do things their husbands don't."

"Come here," Darrian said, leaving no room for objection.

I rose, walking around the table.

It didn't matter that we were in a room full of people. It didn't matter that most of those people looked our way. Darrian pulled me into his lap, tugging at strands of my hair with a purr. "That is not what wives and husbands do, Grace," he said.

To his credit, the waiter didn't look sideways at us as he placed a plate filled with the most impressive cake I'd ever seen on our table. Chocolate and vanilla layers rose a foot high, and chocolate drizzles pooled on the plate. Darrian took one spoon and scooped up a bite, offering it to me.

The only consolation was that our table was in a shadowy corner, and his back was mostly to the room. I took a bite. What did I care about these people? I didn't know them. Darrian tugged at the strands of my hair, fed me cake, and purred, but I could almost see the thoughts bouncing around his head.

"Prince Charming would never go to another person for sex, and neither would Cinderella. The things that happened to you were wrong on many levels. In fact, I can't think of a level on which they were right, Grace. If we bond as Alpha and Omega, husband and wife, there can be no other for either of us. Do you know what I mean?" he said, taking a bite for himself when I refused it.

I sipped my coffee, loving the added flavor it gave the cake. "I don't understand. Darrian, I'm not smart," I answered, relaxing into his vibrating chest.

"Intelligence has nothing to do with this, Grace. You're brilliant. You just have little experience in the world. I'm saying that the Alpha-Omega bond wouldn't allow us to have sex with another. At least not easily. You could be raped, but nothing else. My body wouldn't function with another woman." He took another bite, and it made me happy to see him do so. Maybe there was something to this feeding another person thing.

"What's rape?" I asked, not knowing.

He went so still that I blinked. Nothing about him moved. I'd never known a creature could be so motionless. "Every sexual experience you've ever had, Grace. Every. Fucking. One." He brought a bite of cake to my lips, and I took it, pondering what he meant. It would take me a long time to understand, but someday I would.

We stopped talking, focusing on the cake and our coffees. No one person could've eaten that cake. The two of us struggled to eat half, but we managed. When I couldn't take another bite, and neither could Darrian, he carefully set me on my feet before rising himself.

No one looked as he wove his way through the darkened restaurant with me tucked beside him. We stepped into the cooling Atlanta night, heading to where the car was parked, and were almost there when a figure stepped from the shadows, blocking our way.

"Who's the slut, Darrian?"

A tall woman with dyed red hair cut in a short bob around her angry face glared down at me. She was all lean muscle and severe beauty. "What do you want, Meghan?" Darian growled; it was not a pleasant sound. He angled in front of me, effectively blocking my view.

"I said, I want to know who the slut is, Darrian." The woman had stepped closer, and her sultry voice dropped an octave.

Darrian moved fast, faster than I had ever seen him. He pinned the woman to the wall by her throat, snarling into her face. Her feet dangled off the ground, and her hands clawed at his fingers. "She's not your concern, Meghan, but know that she's a thousand times better a mate than you ever were. Back. Off. I won't tell you again. Get out of my life. Get out of my city. You took my money; you'll get nothing more from me. Come near of us again, and I'll kill you."

As he dropped her in a heap, and she struggled to catch her breath, I turned and ran.

CHAPTER 8

DARRIAN

I'd seen this before, and I knew how it ended, but I refused to allow myself to fall into Meghan's trap. And I would not chase Grace down; I just wouldn't.

I stood glaring at Meghan, wanting more than anything to kick her in the face. But I didn't do that either. Instead, I clenched and unclenched my hands until I calmed.

If Grace and I had been bonded, it would have been more difficult. As it was, it was hard enough, and I understood a little better what had happened between my brother and his wife in our parents'. The Alpha in me screamed to find her, soothe her, claim her. Instead, I took deep breaths and, with one last look at Meghan, I went in search of Grace.

We'd been in eyesight of the car when Meghan stopped us. Walking forward, I scanned for her, hoping she'd simply gone to wait for me.

I found her scrunched behind the tires. She's made herself so small that I almost didn't see her. Her hands were over her head protectively, and her body shook so hard that I saw it from a distance. I scrubbed my face with my hands, sighing deeply as I sank next to her. "I'm very proud of you, Grace," I said, meaning it.

She gave a startled grunt before unfolding her face and turning it to me. Her eyes were far too wide. They showed much more white than iris, and I knew she was terrified.

"Have you ever run from trouble before?" I asked, knowing the most likely answer.

She shook her head so quickly that her hair flew. She met my eyes briefly before darting them left and right, looking for another escape. I reached my hand to her, waiting patiently until she chose to take it. When she did, I pulled her into my lap, and we sat on the ground behind my car.

"Do you understand what courage it took to run? You decided on your own to run to safety, and for that, I am so proud of you. I will always protect you, Grace. You don't need to run, but I'm glad you had the forethought to do so. It's a step forward in your recovery," I said, tugging at the tips of her hair and purring softly. In some ways, she was so unlike an Omega that I wondered, but in others, she wasn't. She went limp against me.

Clutching her to my chest, I got up with her in my arms. Opening the car door, I tucked her into the seat, buckling her belt. As I walked around the car, I scanned to make sure we hadn't been followed. The parking lot was clear, and I slid into the seat, placing my hands on the wheel.

"Grace, I'm going to move very slowly, and I'm going to kiss you, but nothing else." When my hands stopped shaking, I released my grip and turned to her.

Her face was resigned, but I couldn't help it. I hated to touch her with the edge of adrenaline riding me, but I was afraid that if I didn't, things would get worse. I leaned in, inhaling her scent. Grace usually smelled of soap. Not floral, just clean. Now she smelled like fear, and I hated that I'd caused it. Was causing it.

She sat stone still as I leaned into her, forcing myself not to growl. I brushed my lips against hers lightly before capturing them and slipping my tongue inside. She let out a grunt of surprise but didn't pull away as I took my first taste of her.

Her body was stiff as I kissed her slowly. She tasted like chocolate with a hint of coffee and an undercurrent of wine. I deepened the kiss, noting that Grace didn't kiss me back but didn't pull away either.

Feeling my heart pound in my chest, I pulled away and placed my forehead against hers as I fought to control my desire.

Leaning back in my seat, I plastered on a smile. "Nothing boring about dinner out with you," I chuckled, lightening the mood. Gripping the wheel, I pulled out of the parking lot and pointed the car toward home.

Grace sat perfectly still, hands in her lap. She didn't look left or right until we'd reached the garage of The Graydon. It was then that she slowly brought her fingers to her lips. I watched from the corner of my eye as she gently touched them before dropping her hand again. Her mouth was open in a soft O, and she looked more confused than I'd ever seen her.

Opening the door for her, my thoughts tangled into a jumble of what-ifs. I wondered whether Grace ever had a pleasurable physical experience. I tried not to think about her past or the trauma she endured, though it was hard to ignore.

Sighing, she stepped into the elevator with me. She gave a startled yelp when the car rose, clinging to the rail with both hands. I smiled but paid no attention to the behavior since at least she didn't flatten herself to the floor this time. She was getting better.

I opened the door to our condo, letting us into the warmth. The fireplace glowed happily, casting soft shadows across the room. I turned the lights on low. "Helen should've left a smoothie in the fridge for you," I said, tossing my suit jacket over the back of the couch.

"Oh, Darrian," she groaned. "I couldn't eat another bite. That cake finished me," she rubbed her belly, pretending it was rounded.

"Well, if you get hungry, it's there. I'll shower in the guest bath so you can have the master," I said, moving away from her. Her face scrunched as I left, almost like she didn't like that.

"Okay," she said. "Thanks, but I could've waited."

"Not when there's no need." I left her standing in the living room, giving her as much choice as I could.

Turning on the water as hot as it would go, I slipped under the hard streams as it warmed. I gripped my cock immediately, needing to find release. It had been throbbing since I'd kissed her. Then I resigned myself to three showers a day, wondering if that would be enough. I stroked my hand over my stiff shaft, throwing my head back as the orgasm threatened. I delayed it, thinking that would be more satisfying.

I groaned as my spine tingled, spreading pleasure through my body. Grace's lips were so soft, and I wondered what it would be like to have her kiss me back. Gripping my knot so it wouldn't expand, I came against the shower wall. Spasms wracked my body as the orgasm extended; I pulled harder, begging my balls to empty so I could get through another night.

Feeling some relief, I toweled off, threw on a robe, and went to dress for bed.

Grace was in the bathroom, the sweet smell of soap drifting through the air. I pulled on pajama pants and reached for a shirt as the door opened. She came out, her new hair wet and dripping down the soft cotton of her nightgown. Her eyes caught my bare chest, and she glanced away. Helen had refolded the pile of bedding she'd dumped in the corner, and Grace's eyes fell to it.

"Grace, if I promise not to hurt you, can I touch you?" I asked without thinking.

"Pain is subjective," she answered immediately.

"If you ask me to stop, I will. I promise. If you feel any discomfort at all, tell me," I said. How could I teach Grace that there was nothing to fear if I couldn't touch her? I could be nice, sweet, patient, and kind. I could wait for days or weeks. But she'd always be fearful if I didn't show her there was more to life than fear. More than pain.

She stared at me hard for the span of many heartbeats. Then she went limp, resigned to whatever torture she felt was coming. "Lie down, Grace," I said, hearing how husky my voice had become. "Lie down and remember my rules," I finished.

Looking away, she nodded once and lay down. She lay spread, lifeless and limp before me. Her gown covered her body, and her vacant eyes stared out the window and into the Atlanta night. I breathed deep, hoping this wasn't my biggest mistake yet.

I spread Grace's legs carefully, rolling her gown to her hips and leaving her mostly covered. I blew softly over the short hairs covering her. At some point, she'd been shaved, and the hair hadn't wholly grown in. She made a startled noise, reaching with her hands to stop me.

"What are you doing?" she stuttered.

"Am I hurting you?" I asked, letting my breath wash over her bare core. "Be honest."

"No?" she asked instead of telling.

"Move your hands, Grace. If I hurt you or I break a rule, tell me, and I will stop. Understand?" She moved her hands, saying nothing. "Good girl," I whispered, unable to keep the low growl from rumbling.

I ran my tongue up her seam, delicately parting her lips. She was as beautiful there as everywhere else. Her lips met, covering her entrance and hiding her clit from me. She let out a frightened yelp, and I felt her hands move again, only to slowly drop to her sides.

And I learned a lot about Grace at that moment. She'd never once felt the pleasure men can bring, only the pain. I knew something else; I was going to win this war. Maybe I wouldn't win every battle, and maybe I would lose more than one, but I would win. Grace would be fine. And in the end, all of her would be mine.

I slipped my tongue between her lips, finding her bud and kissing it with all the passion and attention I'd given her mouth. Her sharp intake of breath gave away that she liked that. When I swirled my tongue and softly sucked her core, she grabbed the blankets and arched her hips into me. "Stop!" she cried. "It hurts!"

I stopped, pulling back until her body settled. "Does it hurt, or is it overwhelming?" I asked, looking over her covered body and meeting her eyes.

"It...I don't know," she whispered, making brief eye contact.

"Then lie back and let me give you this. It's okay to be overwhelmed; it's not okay to be in pain. Understand?" I asked patiently. "If it truly hurts, I'll quit."

"Yes," she stammered, watching as I dipped my head below her gown and licked her again.

No slick flowed, and I didn't induce it. If Grace were really an Omega, it would come. With time, she would heal from her trauma, and the rest would fall into place. If Grace was a Beta that tested wrong, I didn't care. She was mine now, regardless of her dynamic.

I circled her bud again. I wanted to put my fingers inside her, but thought that might be too much. She was already overwhelmed and confused. I didn't want to make it worse.

So, I kissed her again, feeling her legs open and her body relax. I smiled into her before latching onto her core and causing her orgasm to build.

Her legs trembled, and her hands rested on my hair. She fought not to buck into my face, though I rather wished she would. She let out a wail, arching into me as her clit hardened to a diamond beneath my tongue. When her first cries started, I slipped my tongue into her entrance, using the pressure of my nose to throw her over the edge.

Her body gripped me, spasming around my tongue as the orgasm whipped through her, and surprised shouts and cries echoed through the room. I was glad I'd paid for soundproofing, though I didn't care. Her ragged breaths came faster, and her hips ground into me of their own accord.

Finally, she went limp, and her widened eyes blinked at the ceiling fan. I rose, turning the lights off before pulling her into me. I adjusted my hips so my hard cock would be away from her, and together we fell asleep.

CHAPTER 9

GRACE

I lay in the dark, tucked under Darrian's arm, long after his breathing evened into the rhythm of sleep. I didn't understand what he'd done to me. More importantly, I didn't understand why.

Even though he slept, I could feel his stiff shaft against the small of my back. What he'd done? What *had* he done? It hurt. But it didn't hurt in a way I was used to. It hurt...pleasantly? It made me feel...something? Like the first explosion of hot sauce in my mouth, Darrian made me feel *something*.

I was in a perpetual state of confusion.

He could've slaked the need of his body any time, but he gave me pleasure? I think? Like sweet things with coffee, it was good, and yet he took nothing for himself.

I hadn't even known such a thing was possible; I'd always been a vessel for someone else's release. I hadn't even known I could experience it myself. Somehow, my body wanted *more* as Darrian pleasured me. Even now, I wasn't satisfied.

Maybe I wasn't broken.

What in the world was going on?

My stomach growled, and I slid away from Darrian, immediately missing the heat of his body. He didn't shift when I left, seeming utterly out. The heated floors chased some of the chill away, and I used the remote on the fireplace to turn it on as high as it would go.

Grabbing the smoothie from the fridge, I settled onto the carpet and drank, letting the gas flames warm me. Darrian was a puzzle. Why would he go to all this trouble for a non-functioning Omega? Why would he call me his mate and ask me to be his wife? Why didn't he just fuck me? It's not like it would hurt anything. I didn't understand the world he lived in.

And who was the woman?

She'd obviously known him; he'd obviously known her.

A frisson of something went through me, fleeing when I looked too closely. I sipped the smoothie, once again so taken by its taste that I drank it without taking a breath. My eyes felt heavy, and my belly full.

As I like spices, I've been trying to learn them. I'd gone through the spice rack in the Capitol Building's kitchen, tasting each one. Was this nutmeg?

Definitely cinnamon and vanilla.

Unable to keep my eyes open longer, I put my smoothie bottle in the dishwasher before stumbling drunkenly into the bedroom.

Darrian lay precisely as I had left him. How could he sleep so soundly when he hadn't even fucked me? That's why most of the men claimed to be with me when their wives found them.

My eyes caught on the folded blankets and furs in the corner. Unable to stop myself, I took the basket, upended it onto the bed, and snuggled on top of the materials and into the halo of Darrian's warmth. I fell into a sound and dreamless sleep.

"Is that a?" I heard Helen ask from the door.

"I. I don't know?" Darrian said. I could hear his hands scrubbing through his hair.

"It is," Miss Helen whispered. "I think it would be if she knew how. Yes, that's it, Darrian. You're doing a fine job. Come on, your breakfast is ready." I heard the door click shut over his protests that she didn't have to cook for him.

When the door closed, my eyes snapped open. I looked around, wondering what they were talking about. Perhaps I'd been smiling in my sleep, and they weren't used to seeing it.

I felt well-rested and satisfied in a way I'd never felt before. Slipping into my closet, I picked a light yellow dress that came to my ankles. It fit at the waist but flowed nicely to the floor. I felt like Cinderella when I looked in the mirror.

Then, I brushed my hair, tucking it behind my ears before attempting to straighten Darrian's bed. I'd made a little bed, kind of, but never anything the size of Darrian's. I ended up piling all the blankets in the middle and calling it perfect.

Darrian was leaving when I exited the bedroom.

"Grace!" he said, shuffling to me and placing a light kiss across my lips. "You look rested. I've got an early meeting. Miss

Helen has your breakfast ready; I'll see you soon," he said, smiling as he left in a rush.

I watched after him for a long time.

"Are you okay, Grace?" Miss Helen said from behind me, her soft smile making me nervous.

"Yes, fine. Thank you," I answered, dropping my eyes. I'd never known anyone to just be friendly.

"Come on and eat. Darrian will be mighty upset if I don't feed you. I've got French toast, bacon, eggs, and your smoothie. You're already looking less wane." Helen chuckled as she slid a plate across the table.

She handed me a cup of coffee, adding a spoonful of sugar and a splash of cream. "Darrian takes his black; you'll like this a lot better." She sat at the table, sipping from her cup. "You sure you're okay, sugar?" she asked, eyeing me carefully.

"Yes," I answered, picking up the fork and shoveling food in as quickly as I could.

"Grace?" Helen started. "Sit a little straighter and slow your hand. No one is taking it from you. If you eat too fast, you'll get indigestion."

"Okay," I said, putting my fork down and chugging my coffee. Helen was right; it was better this way.

She smiled, shaking her head. "After breakfast, you're going to help me put on supper, but first, do you have any questions or need to know anything to help you settle in? I know everything seems to be moving quickly."

Questions? Yes, I had questions. I had a million of them because nothing made sense to me, but I wouldn't voice them. I didn't know Helen; she might be waiting for an opportunity to hurt me. Maybe she wanted Darrian to be her Alpha and would punish me now that we were alone. It was too much; I rocked myself, feeling some of the anxiety ease with the motion.

"Grace," she started, reading my mind. "You're okay; I won't hurt you. I'm here to help you settle and maybe be a friend to you."

"Why would you do that?" I blurted out, unable to stop myself.

"Because I would do anything for Darrian, but beyond that, I want to help," she said, pushing my plate closer.

"But why?" I asked, forking French toast into my mouth. My eyes rolled back; it was excellent.

"Because you deserve it, Grace. Did you know your friends told Darrian that you would be better off dead? They talked about ending your life because of your current nature. Darrian refused to believe that was the best thing for you," she stopped, watching me.

I placed my fork on the plate, picking up the coffee and gulping it from the cup. I thought about what Helen said and remembered hearing Lorelei and Eve mention something along those lines to the doctor when I was first rescued.

The doctor talked about how much damage my body had sustained and doubted I would recover mentally, even if, physically, I might be okay. She had suggested it, and the other Omegas said to give me a chance first.

First.

They hadn't shot the idea down.

They'd said Darrian was my last chance at a normal life, but maybe they meant my last chance at life. Helen said nothing as she rose, refilling my plate and coffee before sitting down.

"I recall something along those lines," I answered finally. "They never asked what I thought." I would have been happy watching butterflies and chasing sunbeams in my room in the Capitol building. I'd been mostly fine. Yes, they had to remind me to eat, drink, and bathe. Sometimes I forget to go to the bathroom or brush my hair.

Only I wasn't fine. Despite the food, I was losing weight, and some days I could barely stand in the morning. I'd had little strength for the showers they made me take. Something had been wrong with me. Something that seemed to get better now that I was here.

Looking down at my wrist, I noticed it was less skeletal. Maybe Darrian's feeding me made the food better. "Why would he do this?" I asked, getting to the root of my thoughts.

"I don't know why Darrian did this; I don't think he knows, either. Darrian's broken," she said, smiling sadly at my sharp intake of breath. "He is, Grace. Beneath the money, polish, and shine, Darrian is damaged, too."

"I don't believe you," I said, raising my hand to cover my mouth at my outburst. I shrank down, waiting for the strike of her hand that never came.

"Anyone can be damaged. Meghan did a number on that boy. Maybe he thinks that by teaching you to fly, he'll learn himself. This place?" she paused, waving her hand. "It's all Meghan. Darrian is bright colors and electricity. She neutered him in a way I never thought possible. Yes, he loved the space, but the white? The Gray? That's not him. Maybe you can fix one another."

Helen got up, picked up my plate, and opened the fridge. She reached in and handed me a smoothie. I took it and drank it instantly; I hadn't been hungry anymore until I saw it.

"Who is she?" I'd assumed she meant something to him, but had been afraid to ask.

"She was his girlfriend. They were together for a long time. Thankfully, Darrian saw the light and cut her loose. She started causing trouble in the family, and that's what finally did it. You don't mess with the Battle family; it just isn't done.

"He would have made excuses about the millions she stole from him if she hadn't hurt his sister-in-law and brother," she paused, watching me suck down the smoothie. There were bananas in it today; it was fantastic.

"Two Alphas don't belong together. They're willful and stubborn. To make it work, one will have to bend, and it was always Darrian. But he didn't bend; he broke. He's done so much better since you've come. You being here is helping him."

"I don't see how. I'm useless," I whispered, finishing the drink and rising to rinse the bottle.

Helen grabbed my arm, turning me toward her. She was just a hair taller than me, which didn't say much because we were both short. Her dark eyes bore into mine, shining with sincerity.

"Now, you listen here, young lady. You are not useless. You've given Darrian a purpose, and for that, I'm grateful. Maybe he can give you a purpose, too, and together you'll find those wings. Now come on; it's time you learned a thing or two about managing a busy household," she finished, letting my arm drop.

The surprise of her grabbing my arm faded. She hadn't hurt me; she'd just said her piece and been straightforward, and I trusted her more for it.

"Alrighty then, sugar. This is how you peel potatoes."

Helen showed me the basics of a kitchen and cooking; it was a grueling lesson. Who knew that things cook at different rates and at different temperatures? Helen did; that's who. She constantly talked, overwhelming me with information, but there was a simplicity to it that was comforting.

I learned everything was cooked in bacon grease or butter, and that Alpha males can be difficult. Every time she slipped in some nugget of knowledge about them, I laughed. It was obvious what she was doing. When few others had, she was trying to educate me. Maybe the Omegas tried, but I'd been too concerned with shadow and light to listen. Helen kept it real.

We sat at the table for lunch, munching on ham sandwiches and chips, when I asked her why she was trying to give up her job.

"Ah, sugar; it's not a job. I help Darrian because someone needs to, and I care about him. Darrian was in a bad place; I'm just helping to get it better. But I'm hoping to get some great-grandkids soon, and I want to be there for them, too."

At first, I'd thought she might be Darrian's wife or love interest, but as I got to know Helen, I realized she was ageless. She seemed old as the seasons but young as can be. She winked at me, hopping up from the table with a nimbleness that belied her age.

After lunch, we made bread. Well, she made bread, and I burned it. But by the time Darrian came home, I was laughing, and we had some semblance of supper for him.

"Until tomorrow, dear. We'll work on bread again. Your smoothie is in the fridge," she said with a chuckle before pecking Darrian on the cheek and leaving us alone.

"I need the recipe for that smoothie," I said, placing the last tray of rolls on the stove.

"And someday, I hope you'll have it. That recipe has helped many an Omega thrive under difficult circumstances," she winked.

Darrian stopped just inside the door, staring. Helen gave a little wave, and the elevator doors closed.

CHAPTER 10

DARRIAN

I didn't know what was happening. Our condo was a disaster, but smelled heavenly. Grace had flour all over her, and neither the condo nor she had ever looked better. A genuine smile brightened her face, reaching all the way to her eyes. They twinkled at me as she moved around the kitchen, looking almost comfortable in her own skin.

Where Grace's movements were often sharp and jerky, she moved more fluidly, placing food and glasses of tea on the table. "Everything smells amazing, Grace," I said, dropping my jacket and briefcase onto the sofa. As a little fuck you to my ex, I left them there and walked away.

"Well, that's mostly Miss Helen. If you smell smoke, that's all me," she laughed, smiling as she sipped her tea and stretched her back. "She's very nice," she added, not dropping her eyes.

"That she is," I answered.

"Go on and wash up," she said, shocking me. "Miss Helen taught me that. She said all women say it, so it's okay." She looked nervous, as if asking me to wash my hands might be too much.

"It's perfect, Grace. This is amazing; I'm so proud of you. Thanks for working hard on supper; come, let's eat." I scooped her into my arms, and she gave a sharp laugh.

Settling her on my lap, I fed her from the plates scattered about the table. There was tender chicken in a spicy sauce, green beans with bacon and almonds, and a pasta dish with so much hot sauce that my eyes burned. Grace devoured it as fast as I could feed her.

She hummed appreciatively with each bite, and I had to admit I was eager to taste it too. Not seeing Grace today had been torture. Leaving early and coming late had left me twitchy. Maybe I should scrap the plan to have her help around the house and take her to the office with me.

I could get her a desk right next to mine, and she could do filing or answer the phone. Hell, she could sit on my lap while I did those things. That was her purpose. That was her job.

With her on my lap, I felt better than I had in hours, even with hunger gnawing at my stomach. And God, last night. Never had I tasted anything as sweet as Grace. There was nothing wrong with that girl. She was perfect. I'd jerked off three times at work just thinking about the way her legs spread open for me. Fuck.

"Are you okay?" she asked, sipping from my glass of tea and making my cock hard.

"Yes, fine. Why?" I asked, bringing the fork to her mouth again.

"You're growling," she said, snatching the bite from me. Her steel-gray eyes blinked at me as she ate.

"Oh," I said, unable to think of something more profound. "I, uh, I was thinking that we should change the condo."

"Really?" she asked, a glimmer of laughter in her eyes.

"Yes, really," I rebounded, straightening in my chair and passing Grace a roll. "It's rather lifeless and doesn't seem to fit your love of hot sauce. Let's go shopping, and you can pick out new things."

"Only if you want to." Her voice took on an air of caution, and I wondered what it was about. "I'm quite full," she added. "There's more on the stove."

She slid from my lap, and I missed her warmth immediately. She moved through the kitchen with ease, adding more food to the plates on the table. I watched as she swayed away from me, cursing the need to ease into this. It was maddening.

Once my plate was full, she attempted to clean up. I grabbed her, pulling her onto my lap and tucking her under my arm. My purr came on reflex, and she relaxed into me as I ate. The mess could wait. After years of eating out and having a pristine kitchen, I liked the mess.

It reminded me I was alive and reminded me of home. With eight Alpha sons, the house I'd grown up in had always been a disaster. Caring for nine Alphas had taken everything my mother had, and though our house was never dirty, it was often a wreck.

Meghan had hated my parents. She'd never wanted to visit. Looking back, it was odd that she had agreed to go with me to meet my brother's new Omega mate.

Meghan tried to fuck Jameson for years, but he would never. Maybe Meghan planned to take Lorelei from him; fat chance of that happening. Seeing Lorelei flip Meghan onto her back and bring a switchblade to her throat was the most satisfying sight of my life. I had regretted what happened afterward, but now I understood.

I glanced down, watching Grace's lovely eyes close at the sound of my purr. If Meghan tried her shit again, I'd kill her myself.

I finished eating and regretfully rose to clear the table. I appreciated my grandmother helping with the house and Grace, but I didn't want her working too hard. She was getting up in years, and as much as she loved it, I knew it was taxing.

We hadn't told Grace about our relationship on purpose because we thought it would make her uncomfortable. We'd wanted her to feel free to talk openly if she wanted, and knew that if we revealed who Helen was, she might not. It was a risk. I didn't want her to feel betrayed either, and hoped Grace would understand.

Together, Grace and I had the kitchen relatively clean in no time. For the first time in nearly a decade, my house looked inhabited. It looked like a home.

"Do you have it in you to do some shopping? We can go around the corner to the bazaar; there were still plenty of booths set up when I came home." I took Grace's fingers in mine, bringing her hand to my lips.

She blinked rapidly, not pulling away from me. "Yes, let me just wash my face," she answered, gently pulling away.

I watched her leave, the gentle swish of her dress enticing me to madness. I would taste her again tonight; I had no choice, and neither did she.

We left the condo hand in hand. Grace only half-climbed the elevator walls as it moved, and I considered it a win. The early December weather was unseasonal. Winter was fast approaching, yet it still felt like early fall, not late.

We walked the few blocks to the bazaar, following the lighted paths. Booth after Booth was filled with art, jewelry, quilts, and handmade items. Atlanta had always been a hub of art and culture. Post-war Atlanta was no different.

Grace stopped here and there, turning a critical eye to everything she saw. She passed clothes, shoes, and baubles, not once looking at anything for herself. It's like they didn't register in her brain. At a booth filled with throw pillows in wild colors, she stopped, tilting her head.

"I don't mind the white, Darrian. I don't know much about matching colors, but the white is a better background." She reached out, arranging bright oranges, reds, and yellows into a riot of color. She moved the pillows around until she had an oddly pleasing combination. "Those," she said, stepping back.

And she was right. I could picture all that color against the couch's white and knew it would be perfect in person. "With that rug," she added, pointing to a softer orange shag area rug. "And leave the rest alone."

I looked back and forth between the rug and the pillows and knew she had an eye. It was artful. Those bright pops of color would make the rest of the condo look completely different.

At the next booth, she picked up towel sets for the kitchen and bath to tie in all those bright colors. Without changing a stick of furniture, we would have a new house. I approved of her choices.

I hadn't been raised Omega like Jameson, but I'd had many an art appreciation class in college. Thinking the higher arts would make me more well-rounded and less brutish, I'd taken many a class. I'd hoped it would help my career; it turned out it only made me better at decorating. Then I'd let Meghan run roughshod over me.

I was finding my stride again.

Grace picked out precisely the same colors I would have, and I loved them. Funny how you can meet someone who helps you find your way, not lose it. That was Grace to me. She let me be what I was; in turn, she was growing into who she was. We completed one another. Now all she had to do was realize it.

Arms laden with packages, we headed down the line of booths when she stopped. I followed the line of her eyes, seeing what had drawn them. A silver-framed necklace filled with bright yellow jewels that formed a butterfly. A delicate silver chain suspended the necklace from a black felt square; it was perfect for Grace.

She moved on, but I stopped her.

"I'll take the necklace," I said to the booth operator.

"Darrian, I don't need it. There's no need to spend your money on me," Grace whispered, threatening to back away.

"Hush now," I admonished softly, handing my diamond Coin card to the clerk.

He handed it back with the necklace, "It will look lovely on her neck, Sir," the man said, glancing at Grace.

I had to force myself not to growl; how dare he look at her? He was an Alpha, not a strong one, but I smelled Alpha on him. Placing my hand on the small of Grace's back, I guided her away, noting the tilt of his nose as he tried to scent her. A growl slipped from my lips as we walked away, causing Grace to freeze.

"What did I do?" she said, shrinking into herself.

Forcing myself to relax, I turned a smile her way. "Nothing, Grace. You did nothing wrong. I didn't like the way he looked at you; I apologize. It's rude of me, but hard to help as an Alpha," I sighed. I'd always tried to be a better Alpha, a softer Alpha.

It had never served me well.

I turned her around, slipping the necklace over her head and clasping it. I turned her back, noting how the light caught the yellow gems, making them sparkle. "It's perfect for you."

"Thank you," she said, her fingers rising to trace the wings of the butterfly.

"You're welcome. Did you know that butterflies start out as plain, ugly caterpillars?" I ushered her forward again, keeping my hand on her back.

"What?" she said, clearly shocked.

"Yep," I started. "Then they go to sleep in a cocoon as a caterpillar and wake up a butterfly. It's incredible. It's what's happening to you, Grace. You've never been plain, but you get more beautiful every day."

"Stop," she said, swatting at my chest before catching herself.

"It's true. I want to kiss you. Can I?" But that was a lie. What I wanted to do was throw her over my shoulder and fuck the Omega into her. But I was doing this the slow way. I wanted to teach her, not terrify her.

"Um," she started, sounding unsure.

I leaned down, capturing her lips with mine. She didn't pull away, but didn't kiss me back. I traced her lips with mine, letting our breaths mingle before pulling away.

"I've never kissed before," she said, stopping me in my tracks.

It was the first time she'd offered any information about her life. And what a statement it was. Grace had never been kissed. Jesus. My heart broke for her. I knew what kind of life she'd led before being rescued. I wasn't kidding myself; she'd been a sex slave. But not one of those men had ever kissed her? It was heartbreaking.

"Well, kissing can be fun. If you let me, I'll teach you."

She didn't respond, and we started walking again. The night was getting chilly; goosebumps rose on Grace's arms. She walked closer to me, letting my heat warm her.

In the condo, we dumped our packages on the couch. Excitedly, Grace started pulling off the white throw pillows and arranging the colorful ones. She smiled as she worked, making me smile in return. I rolled up the old rug and set it aside.

When I unrolled the new one, Grace's hands went to her mouth, and she made a soft squeal. "It's perfect," she said.

"Yes. It is. I couldn't have chosen better myself," I said.

"Miss Helen said you like color. I didn't know what I liked until I saw those pillows. I'm glad you like them too," she whispered softly, stepping back to survey the room.

A home was bigger than some throw pillows and a rug, but it was a start. I loved the new look, and it made me happy that

Grace took something my Nana said and acted on it. It also made me hopeful.

Grace went to the kitchen, pulling her smoothie from the fridge and drinking it with a sigh. Nana had sworn it would help, and it had. Grace was filling out and looking healthier every day. The knowledge that old Omega had about life was incredible. I hoped she'd pass it along.

"I'm going to clean up," Grace said, moving to the bedroom. Already, she was making strides. For two days in a row, she'd remembered to shower. I was glad Lorelei and Eve had been wrong.

Grace would be fine; all she needed was a chance.

I trailed along behind her, laughing out loud when I saw the pile of blankets and pillows on our bed. It looked like she had tried to make it but had given up, making a nest instead. The pile was instinctual to her, and I loved it. It was the most beautiful nest I'd ever seen.

I'd helped Jameson move a chair and spotted Lorelei's nest on their bed. It was a work of art, neat layers twisted together. She'd chosen certain fabrics and colors, making the nest a thing of beauty. I liked Grace's better. The blankets were literally piled in no particular order, making me love them more.

In a world of numbers, speculation, analysis, and forecasting, it was nice to have chaos. Of course, investing and the stock market are chaotic by nature, but this was something different. Grace's chaos was beautiful. I doubted she realized what she'd done and wasn't pointing it out.

The shower stopped, and I heard Grace moving around in the bathroom. I walked to the wet bar and poured a lowball of bourbon. A moment later, the door opened, and she appeared.

She'd picked another long nightgown; this one a light pink. It brushed her toes, but was sheer enough that I could see the shape of her legs through it. "Have a seat, Grace," I said, stepping aside so she could reach the reading chair near the windows. "Would you like to try bourbon? This is a vintage brand. It's quite smooth."

She sat in front of me, and I tugged the comb from her hand and set about combing her thick hair. I passed her my glass, watching her sniff before taking a sip.

"Oh!" she said. "That's…spicy!" Her surprise was genuine, and I smiled as she took another sip. "And…and mint?"

"Wow, Grace. Excellent job. You've got the soul of a connoisseur. I had to take classes on tasting; you have a natural talent." God, what Grace could be if given wings to fly. What could she have been if they'd never been clipped? Well, she wouldn't have been with me, and I had a problem with that.

I combed her hair, sinking my fingers into her scalp. Purring to her, I tugged on the tips as I combed, making her go limp. My glass sagged in her hand, and she hummed. Her hum wasn't a purr, but it wasn't far off.

I set the comb down.

Patience isn't a virtue; it's a weapon. I needed to wield it carefully, or I'd lose all the ground I'd gained. My ma was right. There was a negligible difference between Grace and the badly abused mares we sometimes got on the farm.

They wanted to be okay. They wanted to find their way from the darkness they'd lived. So did Grace. She just needed help. She sighed as I brought my hands down, massaging the sides of her neck and across her shoulders; her hum deepened into a purr.

When the glass almost fell to the ground, I took it. Grace whined softly when I left her to pour a second. "I'm going to taste you again, Grace," I said, watching her reaction over the rim.

Her eyes went wide and met mine. "I," she tried.

"Lie down; I won't hurt you," I added, catching the edge of panic in her gaze. "The rules apply. If I hurt you, tell me, and I will stop."

Scrambling into the bed, she leaned against the mountain of blankets. Eyes scrunched tight, she clenched her hands in her nightgown. I drank my bourbon and went to her.

Lying beside her, I kissed along her neck and across to her lips, noting her soft gasp. She'd expected me to go straight to her core and not her lips. I exhaled softly, letting the scent of my breath ghost across her face.

When my lips met hers, she opened for me. She didn't kiss me back, letting me taste her mouth for myself instead. I traced her lips with the tip of my tongue, darting it into her wet heat. She gasped again, her chest rising to mine.

When dealing with broken things, you must take care not to ask for too much. With each lesson, though, you must ask for more. Just a little more. Each time you increase the pressure, they learn to trust you won't break them. You can't demand or harass the creature into giving in; you must make them want to.

I kissed her neck again, lightly brushing her peaked nipples through the gown as I made my way between her legs. Lifting her gown, I rolled it up, exposing a little more skin. I hadn't dimmed the lights, and what I saw horrified me.

Grace was scarred. Badly. Thin white scars crisscrossed the edges of the skin I'd exposed, and it looked like she'd been cut or possibly whipped. My vision tinted red, and I forced the growl at the back of my throat into a purr. I knew it sounded terrible, and I pushed an edge of softness I didn't feel into it.

What had they done to my girl?

Someday I would ask, but this wasn't that day.

I kissed the skin down the line of one thigh and across to the other, feeling her relax into me. My tongue traced her core, and she bucked off the bed.

Grace tasted like heaven, her salty sweetness calling to me. I growled, unable to stop myself, and was surprised when a tiny trickle of slick rewarded my call. I lapped it up, making her moan.

Grace was a miracle.

I went to her clit, sucking it gently as she cried out, "Please!"

"Please, what, Grace?" I asked, pulling away, noting the way her hips wiggled closer to me.

"I don't know!" she cried out, her words ending in a sob.

"Do you want to come?" I asked, tracing her clit with my finger as I leaned back, watching her face.

She was looking down her body at me, her cheeks flushed. "Yes," she stammered, her face flaming redder.

I dipped my mouth to her core, slipping my tongue into her as far as it would go. She cried out again, bucking against me so that I had to reach an arm up and pin her hips down.

Last night, I tried to be gentle; I'd coaxed that first orgasm from her. Her clit was already hard when I found it again, and she screamed as the orgasm ripped through her without an ounce of gentleness.

Before she could decide if it was painful or not, I had licked her clean and started again, teasing her with my tongue. Carefully, I brought my fingers to her opening and pressed one inside.

She gasped, trying to pull away from me. But I still had her pinned with one arm and held her there firmly as I slipped deeper. Her walls clenched immediately, and she groaned, going limp.

I licked her clit, swirling around it as I teased her. I kept my finger still, not wanting to push Grace too hard, but still needing to push her. She pressed into me, taking my face deeper, and upon her invitation, I slid a finger into the knuckle. Fuck, she was wet. She was hot and wet, and her walls clenched my finger beautifully when she came again, tightening around me until I couldn't have moved my finger if I tried. Her body tried to pull me in, and I wanted nothing more than to give her my knot.

"Fuck, Grace. Fuck, you're beautiful." I watched from between her legs as her orgasm took her, and she cried out, going stiff as she crested. There was never anything more perfect. I needed to fuck her.

My cock strained against my pants, hurting from the restriction. I ripped them over my hips, rose above Grace, and flung her gown up to expose her body.

Crying out, she tried to cover herself, but I held her hands with one of mine and jerked my cock with the other, spilling hot streams of my cum across her stomach as I gripped my base hard so the knot wouldn't blow. I flung my head back, growling as I emptied.

When the last spasms faded, I dropped her hands and moved to rub my cum into her skin. I'd never seen Grace's body. Her eyes were closed, and her head turned to avoid me. She lay stiff and perfectly still as if expecting to be hurt and accepting it. She was covered in those same scars I'd seen peeking out earlier. They were a chaotic, haphazard roadmap of every injustice that had ever been done to her.

I purred loudly as I rubbed my cum across her small breasts and onto her brown nipples. She relaxed when the blow didn't come. I purred louder as I moved my hands to her belly and thighs, covering her with her gown as I went.

I was breathing hard when I spread her legs again, rubbing the last of my cum into her folds. Using my fingers, I found her clit, teasing it to hardness again.

"I've seen no one more beautiful than you, Grace," I whispered, watching her eyes open and turn my way.

She thought to argue; I could see it. Increasing the pressure and speed of my fingers, I silenced her with a third orgasm.

As she came, she rose, clinging to me, her body wrapping around mine. She breathed hard and fast, and I hugged her to me as she finished before I laid her atop her mound of blankets. She was already asleep.

CHAPTER 11

GRACE

I had terrible dreams. One minute Darrian was between my legs, and the next, I was being brutalized by one of the many men in the compound. I hadn't known it for what it was because it was all I remembered and understood. I'd just laid there and let him do it. Did that make me a bad person? I never fought them, not once. Or maybe I had, but don't remember that far into my past.

I'd let Darrian do it too, but that was different. What Darrian did felt good; better than good. I didn't know my body could do those things. It was stunning. Was I wrong for wanting more? I'd wanted him inside of me and I'd never wanted that before. Darrian took nothing from me, not like the others. Instead, he had given me something.

But then my dreams turned to nightmares, and everything twisted in my mind. Every time they'd awoken me, Darrian had pulled me to him, purring in my ear, his chest vibrating against my skin, skin that was covered in his cum.

It was a confusing, twisted circle in my mind.

Lorelei and Eve had visited me smelling of male seed. They never seemed to notice or care. They'd explained a lot about Alphas, but not this, and he hadn't hurt me. It hadn't felt bad. He seemed satisfied afterward. In fact, he seemed more pleased and happier than I'd seen once my skin was painted.

He had to have seen my scars.

But he told me I was beautiful.

No one had ever told me I was beautiful.

This was the most confusing thing to happen to me to date. I slept in fits, unable to find peace in my dreams. Darrian held me, purring ceaselessly, lulling me into a dreamless state where I rested.

When I awoke, the curtains were open to a gloomy sky. Heavy white clouds sat on the horizon, and Darrian was gone. I dressed hurriedly, replacing the stained pink nightgown with another long dress in a similar shade. I didn't like my body exposed, and since I'd never had the luxury of clothes, and now that I did, I hated to be without them.

The men always told me I was ugly and that my breasts were small. They would slap them and laugh or pinch my nipples until they bled.

They would grip my face and call me disgusting or spit on it, or both. One in particular liked to slap me until my eyes swelled shut while he was inside me. He had come on me too, but it was different from when Darrian did it. At least it felt different.

Those men had made me feel lesser, like I didn't deserve their seed. Darrian made me feel cherished, like he wanted to cover me in it. Was that possible? Was that a thing? I didn't understand.

I smelled coffee and bacon, but was embarrassed and didn't want him to see me. What if he thought I was ugly? What if he thought I was disgusting? If he liked me, wouldn't he fuck me? Isn't that what men did, regardless?

Slowly, I opened the door, peeking out. Helen moved around the kitchen. Our home had been straightened, and there was no sign of Darrian. On bare feet, I slipped out, wishing for once that I was alone.

"Good morning, dear," Helen said, not looking my way.

"Uh, good morning," I stuttered, moving soundlessly along the wall as I got my bearings.

"Are you all right?" she asked, turning to me with a spatula in her hand.

"Yes," I answered quickly, looking left and right to see if Darrian was around. Dropping my eyes, I waited.

"You look a little spooked; what's happened? Come eat and tell Miss Helen about it, sugar." She turned her back to me, leaving me to decide my next step.

I stood for a long time before coming to the table. Helen slid a plate of food in front of me, piled high with pancakes, eggs, bacon, sausage, and biscuits. To the side, she set an enormous bowl of buttery grits and a dish of apple butter. I ate ravenously, not realizing how hungry I was until I tasted the first bite.

"What did he do?" she asked, eyeing me. "They always screw up somehow; tell Miss Helen."

I sighed, resting the fork on my plate. "I don't know," I answered.

"You don't know? Don't understand? Or aren't sure?" she asked, her steady brown eyes watching me.

"The last two, I guess," I answered as I shoveled eggs into my mouth, hoping she wouldn't ask me to explain. I wanted help, and I almost trusted her, but I didn't want to make things worse.

"What did he do?" she asked again, more firmly.

So, I told her. I told her everything as best I could. It was hard because I didn't know all the words, but I tried.

When I was done, she smiled sweetly at me, putting me on guard. I leaned back, holding my fork between us.

"Alphas are strange birds, dear," she started, pretending not to notice my stance. "They do that thing because they feel the need to mark a person as theirs. He needed to smell himself on you. It soothes an Alpha and makes them happy in a way other things don't. It calms them much the same as his purr calms you," she said, sipping her coffee as she watched me eat.

"But why not just…" I started, unable to finish.

"Fuck you?" she asked, shocking me so that I inhaled sharply.

"I mean, I suppose," I answered, looking down. I'd never spoken like this before, and it made me uncomfortable.

"Have you ever felt loved when you were with a man?" she asked.

"I don't even know what that is. I've felt nothing," I whispered, looking away from her.

"And that's why Darrian hasn't touched you like that. He wants something different for you both. He's learning, too, because he's been torn apart but never loved. In a different way, of course. Maybe he wants better for both of you," she said, rising to refill my plate.

"Alphas have odd behaviors. This is what you need to take from it: they are driven by their need to care for us. It's suffocating. It can overwhelm both dynamics, but they have no control over it, despite what they think.

"They would sooner cut off their arms than hurt us, even though they may do just that from time to time. It's unintentional; they just need so deeply to provide for us it doesn't always translate well. But Darrian will never harm you, and there's a difference.

"He wants to claim you. He wants you forever; there is no going back from that. Remember, if you get confused or unsure that his actions come from a place of love. Even if neither one of you can see it yet. Once bonded, there can be nothing but happiness between you, or he will be compelled to fix it. That is the nature of the bond." Helen got up, moving to clean the table.

I sat, more confused, if possible. How can a bond that you don't want make you happy? How was that possible? But what would that be like? Until Darrian, no one had taken care of me. I'd never been wanted for myself. I'd never *had* anything, and if what Helen said was real, Darrian *wanted* me. But why? When I have nothing to offer, why would he want me?

Darrian had everything. Didn't he? Money, power, and influence surrounded him. But was it me he wanted or just any Omega, and did that detail matter? What would it be like to feel happiness?

I rose, taking my plate to the sink. "What are we making today?" I asked, changing the subject. It was too much. Far too much.

"Well, dear. I want to take you to the store and get groceries. It's essential to know how to shop for the meals you make. We're going to make prime rib, roasted red-skinned potatoes, and asparagus. We'll add a salad and homemade rolls and call it done. I've brought my grandmother's chocolate chip cookie recipe for you, and we'll make those too," she said, making me freeze.

"I can't leave," I squeaked.

"And why ever not?" she asked, turning to me with a critical eye.

"Darrian?" I asked, looking around frantically. I realized something. Darrian made me feel safe, and I didn't want to go outside without him. The thought shocked me into silence, and I froze.

"Grace?" Helen asked, watching me.

I wanted to turn and run because this didn't feel right. Nothing felt right, but then again, I felt *something*. When had I last felt anything? My heart raced, and I felt faint.

"Take a breath; you're fine. We'll go to the store right around the corner. The benefit of smelling like your Alpha is that it will protect you from other males' unwanted attention. Very few will harass a woman claimed by another. You'll be safe. I promise," she finished, reaching for her purse.

"Yes, Miss Helen," I said, dropping my eyes and following her to the door.

"Get your coat," she reminded. "And your gloves," she added, pushing the button for the elevator.

I did as she said and stood beside her, keeping my eyes down. When the elevator doors opened, she stepped in, and I followed, screaming in fright as the doors closed and the thing moved.

I felt exposed without Darrian's strength and support. I didn't like it, but followed the old Omega through the lobby and into the cold and windy street anyway, because she was right.

Darrian was an important man, and he couldn't babysit me all the time.

Maybe the other Omegas were right that I couldn't function in the outside world. I'd traded one cage for another, and another, and another, but that cage was my safety net. Without it, I was lost. I felt safe with Darrian, but he couldn't always be there. I needed to do this; I needed to learn to live or choose to die.

"You can't keep your head down when you're outside, Grace. Look up," she demanded. "It's unreasonable for Darrian to go with you every time you need bread or milk. What if he needs you to get his dry cleaning? Look up and pay attention to your surroundings," she said, walking briskly away from me and forcing me to scramble to catch up.

"You've got to keep an eye out for trouble and avoid it. See those boys over there?" she asked. I turned my head and caught a small group of males watching our progress down the street.

"If you dally, it will make you seem approachable. Do you want them to approach you?" she asked.

"No," I answered, watching the men from the corner of my eye. They marked our progress but made no move to step forward.

"Good, then walk with a purpose, pay attention to what's around you, and avoid problems when you can," she added, stepping smartly off the sidewalk. Her short heels clicked on the marble patio that led to the grocery store. The walk had been quick. As Helen said, it was very close to The Graydon.

"And what if they approach?" I asked, glancing over my shoulder at the group of males watching us.

"Kick 'em in the balls and run like hell. Omegas are quick. Alphas might be stronger, but a motivated Omega can outrun one, hands down. Don't you forget it." She grabbed a cart and handed me the list of things we needed. "Now, grocery stores are laid out the same. The outside square is the stuff you need the most: Bread, dairy, meat, and veggies. The inside aisles usually have other items that aren't staples.

"This store is more expensive than some, but has higher-quality goods. It's also one of the few stores in town that carries almost everything. There's no reason to travel anywhere else if you're uncomfortable. There's also a District bank and dry cleaners on the far wall. You can do this, Grace. I know you can," she said. Her pace hadn't slowed, and she went through the store with a purpose.

She showed me how to read labels and pick vegetables. It was a whirlwind course on food shopping, but it distracted me from my fear of being out without Darrian. She showed me how to tell a bargain from a lousy deal, pick meat by its marbling, and bread by how it squished in the bag.

She explained each meal needn't be a masterpiece and that sometimes sandwiches were perfect. At checkout, she made me use Darrian's CoinCard and pay for the groceries myself with his PIN. My hands shook at the total, but Helen just chuckled and swore to me that Darrian was good for it. We loaded our arms with bags and headed for The Graydon.

If anything, the sky had gotten darker. "Smells like snow," Miss Helen said, picking up her pace.

"Snow?" I asked, not understanding. I looked around and saw nothing amiss.

The men were still watching from across the street, but their relaxed posture suggested they were comfortable and uninterested in moving our way. I had focused my attention on them, missing the danger that stepped into our path.

"So, Nana, I see Darrian is afraid to leave his new pet alone. He had to call in the big guns," Meghan blocked our path. Her eyes glittered as she looked down at me, her white teeth bared in an ugly smile, her canines longer than seemed normal.

"I'm not your grandmother, Meghan. Now step aside," Miss Helen answered, moving into the larger woman's space in a way I never could have managed.

I stopped in my tracks, feeling like I missed something. Megan noticed. "What, sweetheart? Didn't you know Helen was Darrian's Grandma? That's precious. Is she teaching you to be a proper Omega? I heard you're fucked up. Do you lie there while he fucks you? Did Nana teach you how to fake it? They're keeping it all in the family, aren't they?"

Meghan stepped around Helen and moved toward me. I couldn't breathe or speak, and my stomach sank as she grew near. "Cat got your tongue, cunt? That's all you are, you know—a cunt. A fuckable hole for Darrian's cock is all you'll ever be. It's not like there's anything likable about you. He can't handle me, so he'll settle for a bitch that can take his knot. How typical. You know what?" she said, cocking her eyebrow at me. "That makes you perfect for each other; you're both useless."

"Ma'am? Is everything all right?"

One of the young men from the corner approached, his strides long and quick. Despite that, I stood, looking at the woman Darrian once cared for.

"We're fine, punk; move along. I'm just getting to know this little Omega here. It's none of your business." She moved into me, bringing her hand to my face. "I smell his cum all over you, whore. How could you let him do that? Omegas are disgusting. You're disgusting," she said, dragging her finger along my face and bringing it to her mouth.

"I think you need to leave, Ma'am," said the man as he approached. "Are you okay?" he asked, looking at me before pulling me from Meghan's shadow.

"I. No. Thank you, I'm not," I stumbled forward, feeling the first tear fall from my face. I reached to touch it, not sure what was happening.

"Grace, come, let's go," Miss Helen said, reaching for my hand.

I ignored it, walking in a daze toward the doors of The Graydon with tears streaking my face. They'd lied to me. They'd both lied. One of Darrian's stupid rules was that he would be honest, and he'd broken it from the very beginning. I had told Helen things. Things I wouldn't have if I'd known who she was. It was mortifying. How could they do that? They'd worked together to trap me. Again. A cage is a cage, is a cage, no matter how beautiful.

I strode through the doors of The Graydon, taking the elevator and leaving Helen to face Meghan alone. After dumping the bags on the counter, I locked myself in the bedroom, laughing at the thought that Darrian might say he was proud that I took the initiative.

What an idiot I proved to be.

I wonder if he would be proud of my initiative later.

There was no saving me; there was no happy ending with my name on it. There was no fixing Grace, whoever she may be. I saw that.

The others were right; I was irrevocably broken. Opening the doors to the terrace, I stepped onto the polished concrete, letting the wind whip my dress around my legs, but not noticing the cold. It was better this way. Darrian could move on, and I could be free of this life that had brought me nothing but pain.

CHAPTER 12

DARRIAN

I ran. I skipped the fucking car and sprinted toward The Graydon, hoping I wasn't too late. Atlanta traffic would have slowed me precious minutes that Grace did not have.

When Nana called to tell me what had happened, my heart sank. I knew what Grace intended to do, and I hoped I got there in time to stop her.

Fucking Meghan. I would kill her for this.

Flying through the lobby, I slid into the elevator that my Grandmother held for me. I felt the seconds tick away as we rose to the penthouse.

"I'm sorry, Darrian. I had no idea Meghan would do something like that, or I would've never taken Grace from the condo," she sobbed, wringing her hands. "I tried to get in, but that door is solid."

"Nana, I know. It's not your fault; none of this is your fault," I said when I wanted to scream, yell, cry, and pound my fists into the walls. It wouldn't help. I knew that. And maybe I wanted to blame my grandmother a little bit, but how could I when it was my fault? All of it.

The doors whooshed open, and I sprinted down the gallery, feeling the icy breeze from under the bedroom door. My heart stopped. I hadn't gone to the grassy, wooded area below our building, refusing to believe Grace would do it. The frozen air drafting down the hallway told me I was wrong. I couldn't bear the thought of seeing her lifeless body lying below.

On my way home, snow started to fall, and all I could see was her blood mixed with it, her lifeless eyes accusing me of failing. Slamming myself into the door until it gave way, I charged into our bedroom, looking frantically for Grace.

I stopped breathing when I saw her. She stood over the wall on the ledge, her pale pink dress whipping between her legs. She didn't seem to notice the cold, though I could see her shivering from the door. Her face was transfixed by the sky, one hand held out to catch snowflakes as they fell. They transfixed her, and I understood that she'd never seen them. She'd seen nothing of life but bars.

Her eyes went wide when she saw me, her hand releasing from the rail. In one stride, I reached her.

"No! Let me go! I won't stay; I won't!" she screamed at me. Tears frozen in her lashes, she tried to hurl her body away from mine and plummet to the ground as she screamed and clawed at me because she wanted to die.

She fucking meant to kill herself.

Snatching her over the terrace railing, I dragged her to me. Fuck this.

"You will not leave me!" I roared, shaking the glass in the door and holding her thrashing body in my arms as she continued reaching for the edge. The front door closed, and I heard my Grandmother lock it as she left.

"Let me go," she screamed, fighting harder to get away from me.

"No," I said, slamming her tiny body onto our bed. "You would leave me?" I growled, not caring if I scared her, because what she'd meant to do terrified me. She'd wanted to die. I reached for her, ripping the nightgown from her body. Her dark hair made her skin seem paler, and the yellow butterfly necklace glittered in the hollow of her throat.

She was mine, and I wasn't giving her up, but she'd broken the rules. All I saw was red when my mouth crashed onto hers.

"Darrian, no!" she cried, fighting me wildly.

"You broke the rules, Grace, all of them. You are not to harm yourself," I growled into her face, my hands tracing the trim lines of her body. "And you will be punished," I said, dipping my hand between her legs.

"Darrian, you lied! You broke the rules first," she tried.

"I don't care," I yelled, silencing her. "You are mine, and I offer you everything. You will not leave me," I growled low into her ear, stilling her body.

I'd like to say that I stopped there. I want to say that I considered Grace's past trauma, but I did not. Instead, I licked a line down her body, covering her frozen nipple with my mouth.

I teased her peak with my tongue as I caged her body with my arms, then leaned into her, spreading her knees with mine. Her tattered dress lay ruined beneath her, and snow flew through the open terrace door as an early snowstorm blocked what remained of the light.

She turned her head from me, going still, and accepting what I meant to do.

"You will look at your Alpha, Grace," I warned, taking my hand and turning her face to mine. "You meant to kill yourself. Meant to take yourself from me, and you will watch when I claim you. I tried. I tried the gentler way, but I'm not trying anymore if your life is on the line. You are mine, and you were mine the minute you came with me. You will never, ever attempt to leave me again."

She whimpered, slowly opening her gray eyes. The frozen tears I'd seen had thawed and were dripping down the sides of her face.

I growled, loving the way her back arched her breasts into my chest. Taking one hand, I spread the delicate folds between her legs and was rewarded by a trickle of hot slick. Bringing my fingers to my lips, I sucked them dry, holding her eyes.

"This is mine," I said, dipping my fingers into her hot core and bringing them back to my lips. "Mine. You will not try to take what is mine. Do you understand?" I growled again, feeling my cock fighting my pants for escape.

With one hand, I freed it, stroking myself as I stared into her eyes. "I asked you a question."

"Yes," she spat, her face contorting into an angry mask.

"Yes, what?" I demanded as I trailed my fingers along her clit, making her whimper and spread her legs wider.

"Yes, Master." She glared at me, and I didn't care. She understood, and that was the point. Seeing her on that ledge had broken the air of civility I'd fought to build. I wasn't civilized, not in the least.

Maybe no Alpha should claim to be.

My fingers thrummed faster, and when her orgasm arched her body to me, I sheathed my cock into her balls deep, changing the cry of pleasure to one of surprise. Her eyes went wide, meeting mine. I caught the quick look of betrayal she gave before closing me. Trying to dissociate.

"Look at me, Grace. This isn't the past and never will be; watch," I demanded.

Her eyes opened, and she glanced to where we were joined. I hadn't moved yet, giving her body a chance to adjust. She was so tight that I could feel her everywhere. Her walls fluttered on my cock, inviting me deeper still.

I stroked into her, loving the velvet feel of her pussy around my cock. Bringing my mouth to hers, I traced her lips with my tongue, already knowing she wouldn't kiss me back and not caring.

I worked her with my hips, holding her eyes with mine and refusing to allow her to look away. "Grace, I love you," I said, watching the look of surprise briefly replace the one of betrayal. "I've loved you from the moment I saw you."

"You don't know me," she argued, not moving as I slid between her thighs.

"I know enough," I said, kissing the line of her jaw and down to her nipple. "Watch, Grace. Watch yourself become mine. There will never be another for either of us; watch it happen," I demanded, sucking gently as I palmed her breast.

Her head tilted to watch me worship her body. I didn't care about the scars. I didn't care about her past; none of it mattered except that she'd survived it.

"God, you're beautiful," I whispered, enjoying the way my mouth turned her nipples pink from attention. I'd never needed anything so much in my life as I needed to claim her.

Bracing myself on both arms, I pulled away, glancing at my cock buried in her core. I arched my hips, bringing pressure to her clit. She howled, pulling away from me.

"No, Grace. I'm going to make you come. And when you come, I'm going to cement our bond. Do you understand what I'm saying?" I asked, my voice straining as I fucked her harder. Her breasts bounced in perfect rhythm to my thrusts, and her eyes glazed even though she fought against the pleasure.

"No," she tried. "I don't want that. I don't want you." She gasped, her body threatening to go over the edge with or without her mind.

"I don't care. A few minutes ago, you wanted to die. You've lost the right to an opinion," I said, understanding that I sounded like an Alpha.

I was a fucking Alpha.

Her breath hitched when I gripped her hips with both hands, bringing her ass off the bed. I fucked her with everything I had, loving the feel of the sweat rolling down my back and the rhythmic movement of her breasts.

Grace made me feel alive, and I'd be damned if I wouldn't return the favor. My thumb traced her clit, and her eyes widened in surprise, then closed as she shattered, and I didn't remind her to open them.

She gripped my cock hard, her body squeezing mine as she cried out in shock at the sensation. Before her orgasm ended, I picked her up, brought her to me, and thrust into her from below. She was limp in my arms, and I didn't care. Her eyes were open now, watching mine as I gave her my soul.

She cried out again, throwing her head back when the second orgasm flowed over her, and then I struck, clamping on the side of her neck and tearing the flesh away. I pinned her with my cock and my teeth, shouting as my orgasm slammed into me. Burying myself as deep as I could, I felt my knot expand. Her tight pussy milked it, sending shock waves through me as she pulled more cum from my body.

I'd never knotted an Omega.

Holy shit.

The waves of pleasure kept coming, and I emptied more cum than ten men could make into her, and she took it all. With wild eyes and hungry moans, she pulled the last of my seed from me, making my spine hurt.

I collapsed into a heap on top of her, feeling our bond snap into place.

Our breaths were ragged, her sweat mingling with mine as frigid December air froze it on our skin. I didn't care because I would keep her warm. My knot would hold us together for a while. Her body massaged it, coaxing brief spurts of pleasure from me.

I kissed her, not caring that she didn't want my lips. Grace didn't know what she wanted, but her death wasn't an option. She'd lost the right to complain. I kissed her ears, tasting the salty mix of tears that pooled there. Pushing the knot a little deeper, I made her moan as I leaned away to brush my thumb across her clit.

I was rewarded by the instant squeezing of her pussy around me. Pulling her earlobe into my mouth, I felt her body tighten, encouraging my thumb to move faster on her clit.

She was half on her side, half on her back as I brought her a third time. She crushed my knot, dragging another orgasm from me as well. I groaned at the delicious agony of it. Never had I dreamed this was possible. I'd had exactly zero experience with an Omega before Grace.

In my chest, the bond sang, happy and content that I had pleased her so well. The knot retracted, freeing my still hard cock. I flipped her, needing her beneath me again. Burying my tongue in her mouth, I kissed her hard, pulling at her lips with mine. She sighed when I hit bottom, slipping behind her cervix into that pocket made to accommodate the size of an Alpha's cock. I tilted my hips, hitting her G spot and loving the way she cried out for me.

This time, I moved slowly, needing to feel every nuance of her. My feelings screamed as I loved her with my body. She would feel them; the bond would make sure of it. I let her sense my surprise, satisfaction, and joy at how perfect she was.

When I hit the spot again, Grace cried out, gripping my shoulders and touching me for the first time voluntarily. Her eyes flew open and rolled back as another orgasm surprised her. My best guess was that she hadn't known about that spot. Grace hadn't known about a lot of things.

I made love to her slowly, loving every second she was under me. When her legs shook uncontrollably from one last orgasm, I thrust into her, knotting her again, and nothing had ever hurt so good.

Her body still milking mine, Grace fell asleep in the warmth of my arms.

CHAPTER 13

GRACE

The room was freezing, yet I was warm. My arm was wrapped around Darrian's back, and both were freezing cold. Opening my eyes, I saw his head nestled into the crook of my shoulder, his dark shock of tousled hair in stark contrast with my skin. I lifted my head, seeing the wide-open terrace doors, and that a foot of white fluff drifted onto the floor.

Darrian was keeping me warm, but I could feel that he was cold. Slipping my arm from him, I rose, walking to the sliding doors and closing them to the strange white storm. I could still jump, I told myself as they clicked closed, and if I had to, I would; I lied again.

There was a gas fireplace in this room, too, and I turned it on high before staring at Darrian in confusion as his cum dripped down my legs.

Why would he do this? He'd been so angry. Yet, he hadn't hurt me; he'd only made me feel good. I brought my hand to my ribs, feeling the beat of his heart there. It was the strangest feeling, but I didn't hate it. It was like I held his heart in my chest. Where I'd had none, he'd given me his, and now mine beat too.

I couldn't count the times I'd had sex, but I could count the times it meant something. I don't remember my first time, but

Darrian felt like the only lover I'd ever known, and it was scary. He jerked awake, his wide eyes immediately going to the doors before finding me naked and staring at him.

He scrubbed his hands down his face, breathing a sigh of relief as he held the covers and invited me to him. Tired of fighting, I slid in and was immediately rewarded by the warmth of his body. His purr made that comforting vibration meant to soothe an Omega. And it did, I guess, regardless of what I was.

He pulled me to his chest, hugging me. Our hearts beat in time, and I wondered if this feeling was happiness.

Darrian's breathing settled, and I didn't know how I knew he was asleep, but I did. I could feel him in my head now. I brought my hand to the bite at the base of my neck. Darrian had licked it clean more than once, seeming to love its taste.

I'd heard about a bond, and he'd said he was giving it before he had, but I hadn't understood what that meant. There was a tether from him to me that I could see in my mind's eye.

I looked at what it tried to show me. Darrian was happier than he'd ever been. It told me that. He slept peacefully, and his thoughts were pleasant. He had no malice toward me, none. I searched his dreams for ill will, finding nothing of the sort. He'd said he loved me, and the tether wanted me to believe it.

I watched the flames dance on the walls until his steady purr lulled me to sleep.

I was awakened by the feel of Darrian nuzzling my neck with his lips. He was still purring, and sometime in the night, I had turned to face him. Our bed was wrecked from the night before, and the blankets were scattered everywhere. My body was sore in a way it never had been, but I wasn't complaining.

Darrian peppered my forehead with kisses, then rose in one fluid movement, taking me with him. I gave a startled yelp as he lifted me against him, our bare skin touching.

"Hush," he said, tucking me into one arm and walking to the bathroom.

He reached into the shower, turning the water on to warm, before setting me down and going into his closet. I peed quickly, not wanting him to see, before clutching a towel to cover myself.

He walked back into the room, plucking the towel away as he passed and tossing it aside. I kept my eyes averted, not looking at his body. I heard the falling water change as I examined the toothbrushes in the holder and yelped again when he pulled me under the spray with him.

"Don't be afraid, Grace," he said, tilting my chin to him. "I won't hurt you." He brought his hands to my hair, wetting it. "I want to take care of you. It's all I think about."

"But you wanted me to take care of myself," I said, peeking up at him. I didn't recall being bared to someone quite like this, and the feel of it was disconcerting.

"I want you to know how, of course, but I don't want you to need to do it." He smiled, poured shampoo into his palm, and massaged it into my scalp. I tried to stay close to him so he couldn't see my body, but he pushed me away to arm's length.

I looked anywhere but at Darrian as he washed my hair, tugging at the ends and massaging my scalp as he purred. "You can look at me, Grace; I belong to you. You can touch me, and you can certainly look at me. I'm yours. You own me." I caught his smile and could feel the lightness of his heart as it beat in my chest.

For someone who had nothing, being given an Alpha male was alarming. What did I do with him? I could barely care for myself. I'd failed at suicide because I forgot to jump because I'd been distracted by something falling from the sky. Down this road lay madness.

He turned me, and I stiffened until he poured soap on a cloth and washed my back, kneading the knots he found. Purring the entire time, he washed me from head to toe, front and back, and smiled as he worked.

"Why are you smiling?" I asked, glancing at him, then back at the wall.

"Because I'm happy," he answered without pause.

"Oh," I said, looking at the ceiling.

"Grace," he said, his tone more demanding. "Why are you afraid to look at me?" he asked, taking my chin in his hand and turning it to him.

"I don't know," I answered.

He turned, sitting on the bench in front of me, and brought me to his eye level. "Grace," he said.

With a deep, stuttering sigh, I looked at him. His dark, curly hair was plastered to his head, dripping water onto his muscled chest. Massive, light-brown arms rested at his sides, making no move to touch me. Hard, broad muscles led the way to narrow hips like stepping stones, and thighs with not an ounce of fat flexed slightly as he sat.

His cock hung long and soft between his legs, catching my eye. Last night, something expanded inside of me when he came. I hadn't felt that before, and it was probably my favorite part of the entire experience.

I looked away, feeling my cheeks flame red. Darrian called me beautiful when he was the most aesthetically pleasing thing I had ever seen. "You're pretty," I stammered, unsure of the words.

Chuckling, he said, "Thanks, but you're prettier."

"I don't think so," I said, looking away.

"I do." He grabbed my chin, forcing it his way again. "I meant what I said, Grace. Never scare me like that again." His eyes flashed with heat, making something stir in my belly.

"I won't," I whispered, meaning it. I couldn't imagine jumping off the terrace now. The thought of Darrian's heart in my chest ceasing to beat horrified me.

On some level, I knew that was the bond talking, but I didn't care. I'd been nothing and had nothing. I could remember only pain, degradation, and horror. Now, I had Darrian's heartbeat, and even though I didn't understand it, I liked that it was there. Finally, I had something, regardless that I didn't know how to care for it.

"Where did the, uh, it's a knot, right?" I remembered that word from Eve. "Where does it go?" Glancing at Darrian's shaft, I didn't see it. It was veined and large, but there was nothing at the base that I could see.

"It expands when I come. Otherwise, it's just that extra flesh right there," he said, tugging at a patch of looser skin that was a bit darker than the skin surrounding it. "Had you felt that before? I hadn't," he stopped with a chuckle, a shake of his head, and a smile that showed white, even teeth.

"No," I whispered, unable to meet his eyes.

"In all seriousness, Grace. I won't apologize for last night. You're perfect, and I've never been happier. I wanted you the moment I saw you. I tried to wait and make things right, but I'm done waiting." His hands came to rest on my hips. "Are you mad?" he asked, sounding unsure for the first time.

"I'm mad that you lied," I answered, tensing for his anger.

"And I'm mad that you tried to kill yourself."

I nodded my head, understanding what he was saying.

"Why did you lie?" I asked, poking at a muscle in his arm. It felt like warm marble under crushed velvet.

"Would you have talked to Helen if you had known who she was?" His voice was soft through the purr.

"No," I answered, tracing a curve in his bicep that looped into another muscle. Darrian was all muscle and sharp angles, yet his touch on my hips was light. I'd never known a man to be gentle, yet here was the strongest of them touching me like I was a butterfly. I got caught up in the design and flow of his muscles; they were beautifully made.

"And we knew that. I wanted you to ask her questions. It's the role of older Omegas to teach the young. You've never had that. It shouldn't be embarrassing to ask questions, but we knew you wouldn't see it that way. Who better to teach an Omega but another Omega? Nanas and Moms through the ages have been their daughters' teachers. I wanted you to have that. It's my fault, not hers." He turned his dark eyes to me, watching my face.

I nodded once, accepting his apology. I had no memory of life outside of a cage and no early memories at all. "It seems inappropriate to talk about private things with others," I murmured, not looking at him.

"I can see how you might think that," he hummed as he traced the lines of my scars down my stomach. "You were hidden and out of sight, with no one to talk to, and accepted what happened to you as normal because you had no one to tell you otherwise. You don't need to wonder in silence. If you're unsure, ask me. I'm no Omega, but I can help. If you don't want to ask me, ask Nana, or Eve, Lorelei, or my mom; ask someone. That's how it works in this family.

"To hear my Nana tell it, my ma would've died that first year with my pa if she hadn't helped. It's the way of things," he finished. He brought his hands back to my hips, his eyes resting on the bite mark he'd given me. "Do you have anything you want to ask? Have I done anything to upset or confuse you?" He lowered his voice, and I felt his need through our bond.

I didn't answer right away, thinking about his question. Had he? I was confused about his gentleness and why he tied himself to a shell of a person, but I didn't want to ask that. He hadn't hurt me, not even the bite had hurt, and he'd explained that he was going to do it.

I shook my head no, unable to say anything as my thoughts swirled. Feeling his desire for it, I stepped closer to him. Sighing heavily, he wrapped his arms around me and laid his ear to my chest. Something made me bring my arms around his shoulders. I had no reference point for normalcy, but I could mimic his actions and learn.

He sat that way for a long time, his ear to my heart, and I wondered if he heard two heartbeats or one. When his mood changed, I felt it. He raised his mouth, bringing it to my nipple, and I felt his heart race as he licked around it before taking it into his mouth. I stiffened slightly, and he looked up at me through long lashes, not releasing my breast.

My breath caught in my throat. Darrian was a stunning creature, as far as creatures go. Watching, he released my nipple with a soft pop, trailing kisses to the other as I looked on.

"Kiss me, Grace," he said, bringing both palms up to cup my breasts. He pulled me onto his lap so that I straddled him, and I could feel his cock at my entrance, but he made no move to enter me.

With one hand, he brought my head down, breathing in the air I exhaled. Tentatively, I touched my lips to his. I had no idea how to kiss a man; I'd never done it willingly. Instead, I mimicked what he'd done to me and licked along his fat bottom lip. He groaned, and I felt his cock twitch.

Encouraged, I applied pressure with my lips and slipped my tongue into his mouth. His breathing hitched, his chest rising and falling rapidly against mine. I could feel his pleasure, and I deepened the kiss, loving the way his mouth tasted. It felt amazing.

Hot liquid poured from my core, and I jumped from his lap, yelping at the feel of it running down my legs. It felt like I was peeing, and I stared in horror as thick, amber fluid leaked from inside me.

"Why am I peeing?" I shrieked, reaching for the shower entrance so that I could sit on the toilet. In a panic, I almost fell.

Darrian grabbed my arm, steadying me before pulling me back into his lap. "That's not pee, Grace. It's called slick," his voice was reverent as he held me to him. "I'm honored that you released it for me," he said, his purr edging toward a growl. He met my eyes, seeing my confusion. "An Omega releases slick for their Alpha," he started, his pupils going wide. "It makes penetration more comfortable. It also nourishes us during estrous, and now that we are bonded, you will only release it for me, Grace. Fuck," he said, crushing his lips to mine, kissing me quickly before pulling away. "You smell so good; just your smell right now makes me want to come. Look at what you do to me," he finished, pushing me back.

Darrian's pupils almost covered his irises, and his muscles twitched. His breaths were fast and shallow, and I could see his heart pounding at the base of his throat. How could I have done this? "Only Omegas produce it, Grace," he said, waiting for it to sink in.

Then maybe I was an Omega. This was the first thing I'd done that aligned with that dynamic. "It's embarrassing," I said, turning from him and trying to shield my breasts with my arms.

"It's incredible, Grace. Nothing short of incredible. I am so honored and in awe of you," he choked, his words stopping before he moved my arms, bringing his mouth to my nipple

137

again. He kissed it, then the other, before bringing my mouth to his and kissing me harder; I kissed him back. Our tongues clashed as our lips pressed together, bringing a groan from me.

More hot fluid released, and Darrian cupped his hand between my legs, catching it. He pulled from my mouth long enough to drink from his hand as I watched, mortified. He growled low, and my head fell back as an explosion of heat hit my pelvis, making me grind my hips into him. What the heck? I thought, unable to reconcile what was happening.

A river flowed from me, and I felt his cock press inside, one fat inch at a time. "Darrian?" I cried, the orgasm hitting me before his cock bottomed out.

"It's okay, baby," he said, his breathing ragged. "Come for me, it's okay," he murmured endlessly, some words making sense, others not. When I'd settled on him, taking him as far as he could, he stopped to catch his breath.

He leaned me back, holding me with one arm as his thumb found my core. "Grace, if you move, I'm going to cum. You've wrecked me, absolutely wrecked me. Be still a minute," he said, panting as he pressed his thumb into me.

I ground my hips, unable to stop myself. Nothing had ever felt so good in my life. His thumb moved fast, putting friction where I needed it, and I came again, clenching around his stiff shaft. My cries echoed off the shower walls, and he pistoned three times before giving me his knot and shouting so loud the glass quivered.

The feel of his knot behind my pubic bone made me come again, and I screamed, shaking as the orgasm hurt me in the best possible way. I felt my body clench around him, milking and pulling every ounce of fluid from the sack between his legs. It was incredible. I hadn't even known I could do this.

I'd been fucked by every conceivable size penis, small, long, wide, skinny, but none of them had ever brought me pleasure or made my body sing. Had any of those men been Alphas? It seemed unlikely, as I'd never felt this before. I saw spots of light behind my eyes as the orgasm extended, and my body clamped so tightly that he grunted in discomfort.

I fought for breath and cracked my eyes open. Darrian rested against the shower wall, arms loose and mouth slack. His eyes were closed in pleasure, and the bond between us sang like one of the many birds I saw this summer.

Tied together by the knot, I took a moment to memorize his face while he wasn't looking. For the first time, I looked my fill at him and marveled at his beauty and strength. How had I gotten here from being condemned to death? I didn't know, but I was grateful.

"Will you need to do this to me often?" The words slipped out before I could stop them, and I closed my eyes in embarrassment even as I hoped he said yes.

He rewarded me with a dark chuckle, not opening his eyes as he smiled. "Yes, Grace. I will need you often. You will need me too. Usually, an Alpha claims an Omega during estrous, and their needs are satisfied through that cycle. Not that I won't always need you, but the mad, crazy, wild, incessant kind of need I have would have been quenched if I'd waited, but I couldn't wait, and I won't apologize. So, yes. I will need you often."

He opened his eyes, meeting mine. "I need you again already, but I want to feed you even more, and as great as this instant hot water heater is, it may fail soon if we don't get out." He sat up straighter, pulling me to him as we waited for his knot to abate. "Grace, I've never had this. I never knew this feeling existed," he said, his eyes turning serious.

"Me, either." And it was true. How could I have known? "This is different from all the other times," I said, eliciting an angry growl from Darrian.

"There will be no one else. You understand that?" he said, his eyes growing heated and his posture stiff.

"I'm glad," I sighed, relaxing into him. "I don't," I paused, not knowing the right words.

"It's behind you. If you ever want to talk, I'm here. But it is behind you," he said, calming a little. "I want to explain one thing first. Grace, I may do things that seem familiar, but they aren't. This here?" he asked, putting his hand over my heart.

"This thing you feel? Everything we do together is done with love in mind. I couldn't harm you if I tried. I couldn't use you, either. Remember that," he stopped, and I wondered what he was talking about.

He held me until the knot slipped, releasing our fluids down the drain. That gush felt so different from the trickle of fluid left by other men, and I found I was fascinated by it. Where those other times I'd felt nothing at best and dirty at worst, Darrian left me feeling clean and whole.

He rewashed me against my assurance that I could do it myself, then wrapped me in a towel and opened the door to my closet for me before going to dress.

I picked a filmy blue and white dress with a lower neckline so as not rub Darrian's bite, then went about my routine, brushing my hair and ignoring the soreness in the center of my body. I'd hurt there before, and Darrian was right, this felt different.

I should probably know more about the dynamics since I might prove to have one. And I wasn't mad about Helen anymore; if anything, I understood. Looking back, I saw what she'd been doing. She'd been teaching all along, and I appreciated it.

Darrian came in, groaning as his eyes followed the lines of my body under the dress. "You're going to kill me, Grace," he said, pecking me on the cheek.

I wasn't sure what he meant, but he was smiling, so it must be okay. "I'm going to make coffee. Nana is taking a day off, and I'm staying home. There's too much snow to navigate," he said.

"Is that what the white stuff is?" I asked, glancing out the window.

He went still at my words, a look so dark crossing his face that I stepped away from him. He took a deep breath, scrubbing his hands across his face. "Yes, love. The white stuff is snow. It's rain that freezes repeatedly, making snowflakes. The cool thing about snowflakes is that no two are alike. Go change," he said, softening his voice and stepping toward me. "Put on warm pants and several layers. I'm taking you outside after breakfast." He turned, leaving me to change and wonder what I'd said wrong.

CHAPTER 14

DARRIAN

Fuck, fuck, fuck; what had they done to Grace? Jesus. She came from the *mountains* of The Seventh and didn't know what snow was? God. For the four thousandth time, I wanted to go back in time and slaughter each and every person who had ever done her wrong. Every man who had. Shit. I stopped that train of thought, knowing it led nowhere good because I'd done the same thing. In reality, I was no different.

In the kitchen, I put on coffee, noting the lack of mess. Nana had put the groceries away before leaving last night, which reminded me to call and thank her and explain what happened.

She'd warned me against lying to Grace, and as usual, she'd been right. Seeing Grace on that ledge nearly killed me. Never again. She was mine in every way, and my only regret is not doing it sooner. Fucking Meghan.

I opened the fridge, pulling out eggs and bacon. Grace's smoothie sat on the shelf, and I thanked God and my Grandma that she'd made it. I didn't have the recipe, and I didn't think I had it in me to make one. Grace had drained me dry. I took back everything I ever thought or said about Jameson and Lorelei because I got it. I finally got it.

Grace was mine. I'd claimed Grace. Grace Battle; I wondered what her middle name was. I wanted to sing and dance, but my mom didn't teach me. She'd been busy with the next baby and the next. This was big. Bigger than big, this was everything. I cracked eggs and made a hurried breakfast because I wanted to take Grace outside and show her the world.

She came from the bathroom, moving awkwardly in pants. Thinking back, I'd never seen her wear them, but she'd taken me at my word and changed. She moved stiffly, reaching the table before I could set a plate down.

"Don't even think about it," I growled, rushing to plate food and pour coffee into an oversized mug.

Sighing, she waited patiently until I was settled, then crawled into my lap.

"I really can," she started.

"No."

"Okay," she said with a laugh as she accepted the fork I brought to her mouth. How many times had I fed her? This time seemed more significant as it was the first as bonded mates. Was this love? I had to think it was.

In the name of love, I had tolerated Meghan's abuse. This was nothing like what I'd called love then. Looking at Grace was like looking at the sun. It hurt, but the beauty of it outweighed the pain. My heart beat outside of my body in another's, and it was exhilaratingly terrifying.

What I felt for Meghan didn't come close to comparing.

I fed Grace until her bites were sluggish, then handed her the smoothie, arching my brow when she thought to refuse. Dutifully, she drank, groaning at the first sip. That smoothie had saved both our lives. Had my Nana not known the recipe would help Grace get well, both of us would've suffered.

My daily contributions had taken the edge off the need I had to claim her. Grace came to us severely malnourished. Nana said her diet lacked the thing Omegas need most: an Alpha.

From the first day, I'd fed her in more ways than one, and that strengthened the bond we shared. She'd kill me when she found out, but it was worth it. It was all worth it.

I made hot chocolate and poured it into a thermos while Grace tidied the kitchen. I watched as she switched the knife block's position with the coffeemaker, standing back to eye the change. It made me smile. She would settle in. Given a choice, who would not choose to be happy?

I went to the west terrace, digging through the storage closet to drag out an old sled. It was a metal disk, dented from years of use, but it was still fast. Grace waited by the door, giving me curious looks when I carried it down the hall. Hot chocolate and sled in hand, we left, braving the cold Atlanta day.

The walk to the pre-war golf course was short. Time had made Atlanta smaller, not larger. In the absence of destroyed buildings and congested roadways, much of it was easily navigable on foot.

I watched Grace take in everything. She'd stop walking, distracted by the way snow drifted against a building or on a tree limb.

Watching her was like watching a child experience the world for the first time, and I was honored to be the one to see it. Her attention was everywhere, and I had to keep her from walking into the path of a truck plowing the road. I pulled her back with a laugh, hugging her to me.

Snow continued to fall, and she danced, spinning with her arms wide. Her laughter echoed through the empty streets, and I was never more sure of anything in my life than I was of her. Of us.

We weren't the only ones sledding at the old course. While some still played golf, today was a day for skating, sleds, and snowmen. I took Grace to the nearest hill.

"Hop on," I encouraged as she stared at a cardinal in the snow.

"What?" she asked, turning her face my way.

"Hop on!" I laughed, enjoying the way her smile spread at my excitement.

"Then what?" she asked, looking nervously around.

"Sit," I laughed harder, demanding she do as I said. With a sigh, she sat.

As soon as she settled on the disk, I pushed her over the hill. Her sharp cry of surprise turned into laughter halfway down the hill. By the time she reached the bottom, her arms were in the air.

"It's like flying," she laughed when I made my way to her. "Let's do it again," she ran, tumbling through the snow. She fell, spreading her arms wide and making a snow angel, and I wondered if it was because of a long-forgotten memory or something else. Snow angels are instinctual, aren't they? On some fundamental level, we all know how to make them.

Grace jumped, clapping her hands as I readied the sled. The moment it was set, she jumped on and was gone, her shrill cries making my heart settle. I raced behind her so I could meet her at the bottom and pluck her from the sled.

Gripping her under her arms, I picked her up and twirled her as the snow fell, catching on her lashes. Her scarf slipped and fell while her eyes went skyward, and her laugh deepened.

"Thank you, Darrian. This is the most fun I've ever had," she said, bringing her lips to mine and kissing me for the first time of her free will.

"It's my pleasure, Grace. No thanks are necessary." I smiled up at her before letting her slide down my body and onto her own feet. "Come on, let's make a snowman and see if anyone is renting skates."

We played the day away, me remembering a childhood I thought long gone, and Grace experiencing one for the first time.

We drank hot cocoa, made snowmen, threw snowballs, and rented skates.

Grace was a natural on them. After a few stops and starts, she was skating circles around me, and I wondered again if she'd done this before. No one knew her past; maybe she had experienced winter. As the day wore on, the snow stopped and the sun shone.

I watched with amusement as Grace's eyes caught it glittering on the snow. She tried to find the light, making the snow shimmer, and only after I explained it for the third time did she believe that the snow itself was not shining.

When the sun set, hand in hand, we headed home. We'd eaten hot dogs and fries from a stand near the course, but our stomachs were growling again. I planned on making steaks for supper and couldn't wait to share an evening with Grace in front of the fireplace.

I'd never been happier in my life.

As we approached The Graydon, I heard helicopter blades in the distance. Ignoring them, we stepped inside, hitting the elevator button for the Penthouse. Grace didn't cling to the walls or shriek when it rose, and I was victorious.

We entered the condo and were immediately surrounded by the swirl of snow and the thrum of helicopter blades as they slowed. I was the only one with access to the roof's transport pad, and it was something I paid dearly for, even though I had no desire to use it daily. In ten years, I'd used it twice and The Alpha once. I tucked Grace behind me as we went deeper inside.

"I'm going to warm up and change," she said, ducking behind me and closing the door to our bedroom. I hated she was out of sight when I had no idea what was going on, or who was visiting, but she seemed unconcerned, and I didn't want to change that.

Loud pounding at the door dragged my attention away from Grace's departure. "Coming," I said, walking to the door. Checking the peephole, I saw my brother and The Alpha on my doorstep. With a deep sigh, I opened the door and invited them in.

I moved to stand by the fireplace, indicating they should sit. "To what do I owe the pleasure?" I asked with a smile. I so rarely had visitors that it was nice, despite their interruption of the evening. "Bourbon?" I offered.

"Thanks, Bruh," Jameson said, moving to the wet bar. "I can get it. I'll get you one too. You're going to want it," he added. I looked over at him, catching his solemn face.

"What's happened?" I asked. "The girls?" I demanded, straightening to my fullest height.

"The girls are fine, Darrian," The Alpha said, accepting the glass Jameson held for him. Jameson had recently become The New South's Second Alpha, and I was beyond proud of my baby brother.

149

He'd been a late baby for our mother and had almost taken her life when he was born. I'd hated him at first sight but loved him immeasurably since. Out of all my brothers, he was my favorite.

I heard a startled gasp and raised my eyes to see Grace, visibly shaken, trying to back down the hallway unnoticed.

"Grace, come and greet The Alpha of the New South and Jameson, Lorelei's mate," I said, unsure if she'd met them in person. I reached out my hand for her to come to me.

She stood, seemingly unable to move, looking frantically between the men in the room. Her eyes were wide and terrified, and her fingers clutched at her butterfly necklace. She'd put the blue and white dress on again, leaving her bite mark exposed.

"Grace," I said firmly. "No one will hurt you. Come." There was a trigger here for Grace, one I didn't understand, but that didn't excuse poor manners.

The Alpha of the New South was in our living room; now was not the time to be rude.

Dropping her eyes, she came to me with her shoulders slumped, feet shuffling on the floor. "Look up, Grace. Say hello," I reminded, hating the backward step she'd taken in her recovery.

"Hello." She raised her face, turning to where my brother and Lukas sat. She nodded once, dropped her eyes, and plastered herself to my side, practically hiding behind me.

150

"Grace," I warned. Her eyes snapped to mine, wide and panicked.

"Are you giving me to them?" she whispered, her voice dead. She dropped her eyes, unable to look at me.

My heart sank, and I didn't care that I had guests or who those guests were. At that moment, all that mattered was that Grace understood something vital to me. I sidestepped to a chair, sitting down and pulling her to me so I could look her in the eyes. On the inside, I was raging, but not at Grace, never at Grace.

What kind of world had she come from? What God-forsaken, fucked up hellhole had she lived in where this kind of thing happened to her? Not could have, no, not could have. Had happened. We do not fear things we don't understand need feared.

"Grace," I said, taking a hand and bringing her face to mine. "No. They would never touch you, understand that. You are in a room with three mated Alpha males. You are safer here than anywhere on this planet. Furthermore, the only way you will ever be touched by another is if they climb over my dead body. Understand? You're mine, only mine." I had trouble finishing the sentence; I heard my voice shake. The room had gone silent.

Grace nodded once, climbing onto my lap and burying her nose in my neck. I purred for her instantly, stroking her hair until she relaxed.

Glancing up, I caught Jameson's startled expression and The Alpha's half-smile. "Well, things have escalated in a not unforeseen direction rather quickly," he chuckled, shaking his head.

"Lukas," Jameson warned, eyeing my protective hold on Grace, because Jameson would understand.

"It's fine, Jameson. Grace is doing very well. I've never been prouder of someone in my life. We just caught her unawares, that's all," I said, stroking her back. "Are you okay?" I asked, tilting her so I could see her face.

She nodded once, raising her head to The Alpha. "I apologize for being rude," she said, keeping her eyes down.

"Look up, Grace," I admonished softly.

She raised her gray eyes, straightening her neck and exposing my claiming mark.

The Alpha sat forward, getting as close to her as he felt was safe. "Never, ever apologize for surviving, Grace. Not to me, and not to anyone." Lukas infused his voice with the power of the strongest Alpha, making Grace slump against me.

Lukas met my eyes over her head, his eyes sparking with righteous indignation. He'd known what she thought they were here for, but he wasn't angry at her. "Remember one thing, Grace," he said, calling her eyes to his. "None of them are alive, not one. And here you sit, Grace. Here. You. Sit." The smile that broke on his face should have terrified her, but it didn't.

She nodded once, turning to me with a smile of her own. "I'll get drinks," she said, sliding from my lap and moving into the kitchen. She turned her back on us completely as she went.

I leaned back, scrubbing my hands down my face. "She's getting better, Lukas. I swear. I won't let you take her," I said, fighting the growl that wanted to come.

"You're doing a fine job, Darrian. I mean it. Grace looks healthy. She spoke more words in the last minute than she ever has, and she met my eyes. I wasn't sure you could do it, but you are doing it. Good job. I would have hated putting her down," he said, leaning back against the couch. Regardless of whether it was oversized, Lukas made it look tiny.

"We're actually here on official business, brother," Jameson said, leaning forward. "Meghan's dead."

CHAPTER 15

GRACE

The glass slipped from my hand before I could stop its fall. My hand shook, going to my mouth to cover the sharp gasp. Dropping a towel on the mess, I took glasses of sweet tea to Jameson and The Alpha before sitting on the edge of Darrian's chair.

"I didn't do it," Darrian replied almost immediately.

"We know," The Alpha said, running his hands through his hair. It was graying, especially at the temples. I wondered if it was Eve or his job that caused it. Likely, it was a combination of both.

"Jameson spent all night looking at video footage of Atlanta to verify that." The Alpha leaned back with a sigh. "We didn't come until we were sure."

"Who?" Darrian asked, pulling at the ends of my hair to calm himself, not me.

"We don't know yet. We just know it wasn't you or Grace," Darrian's brother said, stunning me.

How could I possibly kill someone? I couldn't even manage to kill myself, let alone someone else. But then I remembered who these men were married to, and the comment made more sense.

"I've traced both of your movements through security cameras during the time of the murder," continued Jameson, leaning forward to match The Alpha's pose. "Cams follow us just about everywhere, but Meghan was in a blind spot. And I think the killer knew that. You weren't the only one she scammed out of millions." He leaned back, looking around the condo for the first time.

"When did this happen? How?" asked Darrian, tugging harder on my hair.

"Last night, around ten," answered The Alpha, glancing at me. "She was stabbed in the heart," he finished, staring hard at Darrian.

"Robbery?" he asked.

"They left the antique Rolex and about a grand in cash on her body," Jameson answered. "It seemed personal."

Darrian nodded and exhaled. "I had nothing to do with it, I swear. Grace and I were in all night."

"We believe you, but we still have to look into it. It could be a contract killing," The Alpha said, his rich accent sounding much different from Darrian's. "Half of the New South had motive, Darrian. We'll find them. Unfortunately, it happened not long after your run-ins with her, so we have to look at you."

Stiffening behind me, Darrian answered, "You know about that?"

"I know everything." The Alpha of The New South leaned forward, staring us both down. "It's my job. Is there anything you want to add?" His grin challenged us to speak.

"No," Darrian replied, not sounding nervous. If I had my way, I would've run down the hall and hid in a closet.

"Don't worry about it, Darrian; we'll figure it out," Jameson said, looking relaxed.

"We were about to make supper," Darrian said, sliding me off his lap and rising to his feet. "Care to join us?"

I felt my mouth drop open. Is that what manners were? Someone accuses you of murder, and you invite them to supper? I would come to learn that you do, indeed, invite them to supper. After all, it's still the South, and some things never change.

"Thanks for the offer, but no," The Alpha said, rising to his feet as well. "We need to follow up on a few things. Though there isn't any footage of the actual murder, we've identified people from the video footage in the surrounding areas and need to talk to them. Hopefully, someone saw something. Alpha females aren't common; someone should remember her."

"Grace, it's good seeing you," Jameson said, standing next to The Alpha. I had to force myself to be calm and smile. I'd been surrounded by men before, but never so many this large, and it was frightening. "Ma will expect a visit before too long; she's champing at the bit to get her hands on you," he finished with a chuckle. Walking to the door to open it for The Alpha.

"I," I stammered, looking to Darrian for guidance. He gave an encouraging smile, nodding his head. "I look forward to it," I finished, willing my voice to be stronger than I felt.

Jameson's face lit up as he looked at me, leaving me confused. "Perfect," he said, beaming. "I'll let Lorelei know you're doing okay," he finished.

They left us in peace. The helicopter blades kicked up a whirlwind of snow, blanketing the floor-to-ceiling windows surrounding the condo in white.

Darrian stood by the fire for a long while, looking into the flames as he sipped drink after drink.

"I'm sorry she's dead," I tried, unsure what decorum called for under these circumstances.

"I'm not," he answered immediately. "I should be, but I'm not." He sighed heavily, tipping back the last of his bourbon and pouring another. "Care for a drink?" he asked, offering me his. "Go ahead, Grace." He held the glass to me, and I took it, sipping the amber liquid delicately.

It hit me like fire, and I remembered I liked it. Like hot sauce without the heat, it had a kick to it that called to me. "It's good," I said, handing it back.

"Let me pour you a glass," he said, moving to the wet bar to pour me a second glass before refilling his own.

"Thanks," I said, watching him move back to the fireplace. He wasn't unaffected by Meghan's death. If he had been, I would have thought less of him. Worry lines etched his somber face, and his body was stiff as he stood staring at the flames. "I'll start supper," I said, moving to leave him with his thoughts.

He grabbed my arm, jerking me to his body, where he gripped me. I gasped as he buried his nose in my neck, growling angrily. I went limp, not understanding the situation but understanding that now was not the time to argue.

Snaking my arm around his neck, I hummed to him. I didn't understand my actions, not even a little bit, The bond called for it, and I answered. He calmed, and his growls stopped.

"You're a good man, Darrian," I said, continuing my hum. It sounded almost like his purr, but softer, gentler.

"Jack Daniels disagrees, Grace," he whispered, biting up the side of my neck and making me shiver. "I've tried so hard to be better, to be different. I wanted to be something more than bundled Alpha instincts and aggression, but in the end, that's all I can be; I'm sorry. I really am. You should've been allowed to heal before I forced my whole ass self on you. I wanted you to be whole so that nothing I did would scare you, but I can't stop. I can't be something I'm not," he said, sliding my dress over my hips and backing me toward the couch. "And I'm about to scare you. I know it, but I can't stop myself."

"Darrian," I gasped when my knees hit the edge of the couch. "Listen," I said, understanding something I hadn't until then. "I'm here, safe, and with you, and I'm not leaving. Meghan didn't want your protection; she didn't think she needed it, but I accept it. I accept you, Darrian. I know who you are, and you don't scare me," I lied a bit, continuing my soft humming.

My past said I should be terrified of the glint in his eyes and the determined set to his jaw. My past said his tight grip on my hips would lead to nothing but pain. But my present knew better. Even if he threw me down and fucked me, it would be different. I accepted that, too, but didn't put it into words. "Maybe I'll never completely heal, Darrian, or be whole. How can I heal wounds I don't know exist? But I trust you, and I understand," I said, looking up at him. My heart pounded as the bond urged us toward peace. "If you need something, I'll try to give it. I'm not Meghan; you have nothing to prove to me," I finished, watching the spell on Darrian break.

He breathed deeply, taking a step back. Scrubbing his hands down his face, he pulled me into a gentle hug.

"Fuck, Grace. I'm sorry."

"Don't be. You loved her. You were together for a long time. If you weren't affected, I'd be worried," I said, stepping back to catch the look of relief that crossed his face. "I'm starving. Your grandmother gave me a steak rub recipe I'm dying to try."

Darrian ducked his head, looking sheepishly, just as my stomach growled loudly, and we laughed, breaking the seriousness.

"Come on; let's eat."

Darrian grilled steaks with the rub I made while I fried potatoes and onions in a pound of butter per Miss Helen's instructions. I roasted Brussels sprouts in garlic and parmesan, and no restaurant had ever served a better meal.

Sitting at the table while the storm's renewed rage blew snow in front of the windows was the most peaceful moment I'd had in my life to date. Shadows from the flames flickered on the wall, and the absolute silence of the building settled me in a way I'd never been settled before. The world had been whittled down to two beings: Darrian and me.

The compound in the Seventh was always loud. Always, there was fucking, fighting, or both. Children cried or laughed at intervals throughout the day and night. Screams sounded at all hours because I wasn't the only woman held there, just the quietest one.

At no time was the place silent. Over the months since my rescue, I'd learned to count. I'd tried to count the men and women who took my body and found I couldn't. And in a house that large, there was never peace.

I smiled at Darrian; I couldn't help it. Outside, the wind blew, and snow piled up, but inside? Inside, there was peace.

Something in my heart eased. Some part of my mind gave in to an idea it had earlier refused. Darrian was my mate. He was mine. And The Alpha was correct; I had survived. I couldn't say if any of the other captives had. I remember nothing of that day but smoke, fire, and Eve.

But me?

I survived.

I felt tears slip down my face, confused about why my eyes were watering.

"Grace?" Darrian asked, his alarm disturbing the abyss I'd fallen into. "What's the matter?"

"Nothing," I answered, growing confused when he stiffened.

"Nothing rarely means nothing, Grace," he said, scrunching his eyebrows together and reaching for my hand. He'd fed me from his plate, but after I'd moved to sit across from him, enjoying the way the firelight danced on his skin.

Between Darrian and the snow, I was surrounded by breathtaking beauty. The condo was perfect, and everything felt so right. I had wanted to take it all in, and that's hard with almost seven feet of Alpha male wrapped around you. Darrian hadn't complained that I sat in the chair across from him when he rose to fill our glasses.

"Nothing, I swear. I've had a great day."

"But you're crying."

"I don't understand it either," I laughed, tossing my head back and finishing my bourbon.

I felt light and happy. Why was I crying? Was I drunk? I'd never been drunk and wasn't sure what it felt like, but I felt like myself. Maybe a little warm and fuzzy, but myself. I chuckled again.

Darrian smiled, and my heart beat faster. My gaze settled on his fat lower lip, and I stared at it longer than was polite. Yep, definitely drunk. His smile broadened when I glared at my empty glass.

"Well," I said, clearing my throat and not knowing what to say next.

"It's late," Darrian said, his eyes twinkling with merriment. "I'll clean this mess up tomorrow. Let's get you to bed."

CHAPTER 16

DARRIAN

Grace was drunk, and it was adorable. I hadn't noticed it happen. She'd been sipping bourbon since Jameson and Lukas left; she kept sipping and sipping. It snuck up on us.

It was the giggle that clued me in, then the tears, and then the giggle again. Grace rarely laughed, but she never giggled. The radiant smile never left her face, and I was so in love that my heart hurt.

Tonight, she purred for me. Some dumb Alpha switch had flipped, and I was getting ready to bend her over the couch and prove I could protect her by fucking her. I mean, how does that even make sense? I couldn't stop myself even though I could see it coming.

But Grace stopped me. With her honest words and broken purr, she stopped me. Her soft nature and calm soul took away whatever venom I wanted to fill her with.

I thought about Jameson and Lorelei in that fucking barn. I knew what had happened. We all did, and I was grateful that Grace stopped me from doing that to her. Again. Would it happen someday? I was sure it would, but we were both too fragile to have it happen now. Our day had been perfect.

Almost perfect.

I wasn't sad Meghan was dead, but Grace was right. I couldn't protect Meghan, and that's what hit me. Grace thought I was a decent man who mourned her death, but in that, she's mistaken. I would've stabbed that bitch in the heart in a second if I'd had the chance.

Meghan put Grace on the ledge of our balcony. She'd done or said something that made Grace want to die. I would have happily murdered her, but someone beat me to it.

While I'd been bending Grace to my will, someone else had gotten their revenge. I'd planned on killing her; I just hadn't gotten past the planning stages, but in this, the killer did me a favor because I'd have gotten caught and put to death, leaving Grace alone.

Watching the way the firelight played across her pale skin, making her gray eyes appear larger, I couldn't imagine not being there for her. She was smiling at everything and looked happy.

Maybe she was right, and she'd never be whole or fixed, but then who was? How many adults reached our age intact? Not many; I certainly wasn't.

Had she ever been happy? I wondered, knowing the answer. The gaunt, haunted look on her face in that courtyard told me the truth. But her eyes weren't empty now.

"Are you happy?" I asked, unable to stop the words from coming.

Her face fell and then lifted again as she seemed to think about it. "Maybe I am," she started, taking my glass of Jim Beam and finishing it. "I haven't been unhappy since my rescue. Maybe content to be nothing, feel nothing. I'm not sure I've ever been happy; there's always been an edge of fear. But today, I experienced happiness without fear, and that is different," she finished.

She rose from her chair, reaching for my hand. "It's been a long day," she said, mirroring my words. "Let's go to bed."

Instantly, I was on fire. The need to have her was back, stronger than it had been when I threatened to bend her over the couch. My smile dropped, and my cock hardened.

"Grace," I growled.

"It's okay; come on," she smiled again, pulling me down the gallery toward our bedroom. She was still giggling, and I hoped she didn't hate me in the morning.

Again.

With Alphas, it's always again.

In our bedroom, she pulled the dress over her head, exposing her body to me. She'd never willingly done such a thing, and I'd never asked her to. It showed a level of trust I hadn't earned.

"Don't rip this one. I like it," she laughed, reaching behind her back to unclasp her bra while I watched, stunned.

Grace was happy, joking, and undressing for me. I needed to get her drunk more often. This was a glimpse of who Grace was before she'd been broken and a peek at the woman she might become. I didn't like this version more, but it gave me hope that someday she'd be comfortable in her skin.

I stepped forward, palming her breasts in my hands. Lowering my lips to her hair, I kissed it, inhaling the scent of her soap. Kissing her neck, I growled for her, loving the way she bent into me.

"Darrian," she purred, and I loved the sound of my name on her lips.

"Mmmhmm," I responded, unable to speak actual words.

"Can I?" She stopped, going stiff.

"Can you what, Grace? The answer is already yes," I said, scenting her slick.

She stepped back, pulling my shirt over my head, and the mood changed. I'd been ready to rut her like the beast I was, but the soft look of wonder on her face stopped me.

"You're beautiful," she whispered, running her hands down the planes of my bare chest.

"You're drunk," I laughed, clutching her hands in mine to stop her delicate torture.

"Maybe, but it doesn't change the truth," she smiled at me through her lashes, and I was gone. I was supposed to save her, but I lost myself instead, and I'd never been happier about anything in my life.

"You may have hit your head sledding," I said, capturing her lips.

"I think I'm perfectly fine," she said, pulling her hands free and resuming her perusal of my chest. She was focused on the definition between each muscle, and the feel of her hands was killing me.

"That's what they all say until they wake up with a hangover," I chuckled, bringing her face to mine with a finger. I kissed her deeper, loving the way her mouth tasted.

"No," she said, stepping back from me.

I quirked an eyebrow. "What did you say?" I asked, lowering my voice in challenge. Her knees nearly buckled, her eyes rolling back in her head.

I chuckled, peppering her forehead with kisses. She'd told me no, and my heart burst with pride for her.

"No," she repeated, smiling at the way the word sounded on her tongue. "I don't think I've said that word before, not in this context," she added, pulling away from me. My pride melted into sadness, tipping my head back and closing my eyes.

"I didn't mean to say that," she said, tracing her hands lower. Her fingers brushed the button of my jeans, and I groaned. "I've never touched a man because I wanted to. Let me touch you. Please," she added, looking worried.

"You never have to ask, Grace. I'm yours, all of me. I'm not ashamed of your past. Don't be afraid of telling the truth; it changes nothing." Dropping my hands to my sides, I stilled as she fumbled with my belt. Once she got it undone, she focused on my jeans' button, struggling to work it.

I wanted to help her, but she'd asked to do something she'd never done before, and I couldn't take that away from her. The glorious smile at her success faded when she pushed my jeans down, and my cock sprang free.

Jeans forgotten, she retraced my chest slowly to where my cock throbbed for her. Moisture beaded on the head, and it was all I could do not to throw Grace on the bed. She gripped me lightly, causing a groan to slip from my lips.

"Will you?" she started; her voice was so low that I struggled to hear her.

"Anything."

Her eyes were wide and damp, making me wonder why she was crying again. "Lie down," she said, her voice stronger this time. Pride surged, and I did as she asked, kicking off my jeans as I lay back on the bed.

Meghan had controlled our sex life. I got what she gave me, which wasn't much. I'd lain down at her command hundreds of times, possibly thousands, but it had never felt like this.

Grace watched with rapt attention as I adjusted her pile of blankets to accommodate my size. She hummed appreciatively as I moved, her eyes catching on my muscles. I'd never been admired before, and her appreciation did something.

Grace and I weren't much different, now that I think about it.

When I was settled, she stood by the bed, her eyes touching me everywhere. Taking her small hand, she brushed my cock, making my hips buck to her. The dark chuckle she let out made me look at her through half-lidded eyes. She was enjoying this.

I tilted my head, breathing in the smell of her arousal. Her bare legs glistened for me, and I marveled at how far we'd come.

She crawled forward, running her hands down my thighs, tentatively squeezing my muscles. But her eyes caught on the head of my cock and the fluid dripping from it.

"Grace," I growled, unable to keep the need from my voice.

"I know. Please, just a few more minutes." Her voice shook, but for a different reason than it had earlier.

She brought her mouth toward me so slowly that it was painful to watch. Needing to do a thing and wanting to are sometimes different. "Grace," I whispered. "You don't have to."

"Please," she choked, unable to take her focus off my groin. Tears fell from her unblinking, impossibly wide eyes to land on my skin.

Her lips touched my crown, and it was all I could do not to finish on her face. "Fuck, Grace. Fuck," I cried, gripping the blankets to keep from bucking into her. I heard fabric tearing and didn't care.

I felt her hot tongue lick the fluid off my tip, her body jolting in surprise. Her face snapped to mine, her eyes pinning me immediately.

"You've been withholding information," she said with a crooked smile.

"In my defense, I withheld nothing. I gave you everything I had," I chuckled. "I just wanted you well, Grace."

She smiled, shaking her head, and the spell was broken. Whatever fear she'd fought was gone, dissipating like smoke.

"Mmhmm. I'm going to ask my legal counsel if that's true." She laughed, giving my cock a tentative stroke.

I groaned, and again the mood changed.

Her smile fell, and her eyes went back to where I lay painfully stiff under her hands. Her attention was killing me, but she needed something, and I would give it to her. Maybe this was a step in her recovery I hadn't counted on. It didn't matter. She needed; I would give.

She brought her mouth to me again, her action more sure. She moved her hand so she could take me deeper, and my soul left my body.

And here's one of my darkest secrets. I'd only ever had one blowjob in my life, and I'd paid for it. Meghan refused to lower herself to touch my cock unless it involved her pleasure. She used my body for her own ends, and if I came, fine. If not? Who cared? Not Meghan.

One night at a bar, Meghan had left with another man, and I couldn't take it. I'd paid a Beta prostitute to give me the one thing I'd never had. I could've had sex with her, but the blowjob seemed less personal in theory and made me feel better about the transaction.

I'd been wrong.

That woman's mouth on me was the most personal thing I'd ever experienced, and Grace's mouth even more so. Her strokes were tender as she kissed me in a place some see as dirty. I was in awe as I watched her head rise and lower on my cock. Her eyes rolled back, and she swallowed all the pre-cum I leaked, her groans matching mine.

Then she found her rhythm, and my cock hit the back of her throat and continued deeper without pause. I bucked, unable to help it. I'd heard Omegas didn't have a gag reflex, but I didn't understand what that meant.

Now I did.

Holy shit.

"Grace. Grace, stop. Please. I'm going to," I cried out.

Doubling down on her efforts, she crouched over my body possessively and made her lips hit the close-cropped patch of hair at the base of my cock, and I was gone. Done.

The orgasm ripped through my body, and I roared, shaking the walls with the intensity of it. Her hand shot to my knot and squeezed it to the beat of my spurts, and Grace swallowed with a cute little growl.

She kneaded my cock like a kitten looking for milk, and I gave her all that I had. When the last spasms faded, she collapsed, our bodies a slobbery, slick mess.

"That was," I started, letting the words fade away. There were no words. I had nothing.

"Incredible," she said, shocking me.

I fought to lift my head from the pillow, looking to see if she meant it. Grace was sprawled across my lap, her face shiny with the mess we'd made. Her pupils were blown, and a goofy smile graced her lips.

She giggled when she caught me staring. Then she giggled more, and the giggle rolled into a full-blown laugh. She snorted, scaring herself, which made her laugh more.

"Is there bourbon in your cum?" she asked, her earnest expression making me chuckle.

Grace was cum drunk and bourbon drunk. Nothing had ever been cuter.

"Uh, no," I tried.

"Bullshit! Nutmeg, vanilla, cinnamon, and bourbon," she laughed, nuzzling my cock with her cheek. "I know my spices," she added, rubbing the other side of her cheek on me. "You've gotten me drunk. Twice."

"Grace, your milkshakes had a hundred times less than what you graciously ingested a few moments ago." I smiled down at her, loving her joyous expression. I took my hand and massaged her head. "There is a reason they call it Cum Drunk."

"I've never heard that term," she insisted, taking my soft cock into her mouth, making it twitch.

"Of course you haven't," I sighed as she resumed nuzzling my cock and giving it gentle nips. "Well, now we know."

I tried to pull her to me, but she dug in, growling her little Omega growl and refusing to release my cock from her mouth. It was fucking adorable.

"I want something," she said, cocking her head to the side and looking up at me. She was blinking too rapidly and looking confused.

"What, love?"

"I don't know," she said, her eyebrows narrowing so that they touched.

She crawled up my body, burying her face in my neck, inhaling, nuzzling there too, marking me with our combined scents. She rubbed her face along mine, and I lay still beneath her. Grace was all animal instincts at that moment that neither of us understood.

It wasn't until she started chewing on my shoulder that I figured it out.

"Grace?"

She grunted her response, continuing to bite a line along my shoulder.

"Grace, I don't think you should do that right now. I'm yours. I'll always be yours, but you should be clear-headed when you do that."

"What am I trying to do, Darrian?" she purred, rubbing both sides of her face and neck on my chest as she ground her pussy into my hip. She looked up, blinking. "What?" she asked, tilting her head as she awaited an answer.

"You'll make the bond stronger, Grace. I don't want you to do it now and regret it later," I answered, ducking the question.

Her hand slid to her neck, covering the bite I'd given her. "Can it be broken?" she asked, concern etching her features.

"No."

"Then shouldn't it be as strong as possible?" she asked, causing me to look away.

God, this woman. She'd accepted everything without a fight. I'd fed her, bathed her, and loved her. I'd forced my body and a bond on her; she'd blinked at none of it. And here she was, asking why the bond shouldn't be stronger. I was trying to be noble, but that ship had sailed long ago, if I'm honest.

On a fall night not long ago, I talked to Jameson about the grace of Southern women as if I understood it. Southern women are genetically stronger, in my opinion. Not that I've met women from other countries, but how can they not be? They have to deal

174

with Southern men. Do I understand them? Hell, no. Why do they put up with us?

Southern men are driven, prideful, and cocksure. They are loyal to a fault and vicious when backed into a corner. Add to that the Alpha gene, and Southern women learned grace early in their evolution. That grace is then genetically passed from mother to daughter.

Grace was acting on pure instinct. Maybe she'd had a mom who loved her and taught her things, but those memories were gone now. She sat on my lap, watching my face as my cock grew hard beneath her.

She ground into it again, throwing her head back at the sensation.

I flipped her, putting myself between her legs. I didn't need to growl to incite her slick. It had poured freely while she sat on me. She watched me like a predator, and I knew the high of her Alpha's cum hadn't faded. Pupils still blown, she stared me down as she ground into me.

Sheathing myself in her, I thrilled at the cry she gave when my cock hit bottom. I crushed her lips with mine, needing her.

"I can't be gentle, Grace. Don't hate me in the morning," I said, withdrawing from her only to slam right back in. She'd forgive me. After everything I'd done, she'd forgive this.

CHAPTER 17

GRACE

The feel of Darrian sliding into me was exquisite, and I abandoned myself to it, giving in to the building orgasm. It'd been building for a long time. Having Darrian in my hands and mouth was one of the most empowering moments of my life. Who would have thought?

I wasn't even mad that he'd been sneaking cum into my milkshakes. It meant he cared. No one had ever cared. Darrian wanted me well, whole, and happy, but more importantly, he wanted me.

He'd said he couldn't be gentle, but what he didn't understand and what I would never tell him was that he couldn't possibly hurt me. Not with sex.

He was right when he said everything that happened between us would be different. It was. But that didn't mean my body couldn't handle what he needed to give me. It did, however, mean that now I enjoyed it.

His cock slipped behind my cervix, and once it hit that spot, I fell apart, coming hard. I cried out, arching into him as my body begged for more. It clamped so tight on him that he grunted when he tried to slide out.

Panting, I pulled at him as I tried to get to his lips. I needed him. I needed.

He'd said I would, but nothing could warn me about the depth of that need. I fought to pull him further in, scratching at his back and hips. He put his hand on my throat, squeezing it lightly until I relaxed for him, my body opening up. How can that feel good? I didn't know, but it did. It does.

When I'd caught my breath, relaxing into him, he lowered his lips to mine, kissing me gently. "I love you, Grace. Don't forget that."

I didn't understand until he flipped me to my knees, teasing my back entrance. I stiffened, reminding myself what he'd said and what I knew. He couldn't hurt me, and he couldn't use me.

"I need all of you, Grace. I need it all. There can be only me. Everywhere." He reached between my legs, cupping that slippery fluid in his hands and rubbing it on me.

His cock slid in, rounding my pack with pleasure. And when his hand found my clit, urging me to come in a position that only ever meant pain, I let go and didn't fight.

When he was buried to the hilt, his cock touched a spot I'd not known was there, urging me to push against him for more. I gasped. Riding him harder, I made his cock hit that spot hard until I came. His fingers on my clit and the feel of him buried in me made it more intense than anything I'd felt.

I cried his name. Then the only noise I could make was a long, pained grunt. I stopped breathing, and my heart quit working. I well and truly died.

When I came to, Darrian was knotted in the deepest parts of me. It didn't hurt to have his knot there, not at all. If anything, it felt incredible- different, but incredible. He was purring as he rubbed my back, and I hated that I'd missed his orgasm.

We lay nestled together, his front to my back. Between us, the bond sang. It was contented and happy, but I could feel that it wasn't quite right.

Something was wrong.

My heart sped up, and my nipples tingled. I was so thirsty.

My respiratory rate climbed, and my skin hurt.

"Darrian?" I asked, well and truly frightened.

"Yeah, love?" he answered, his voice slurred with satiation.

"Darrian?" I repeated, unable to get more words out.

His knot abated. I groaned as I felt his fluids leave me. They were mine, and I needed them.

The growl that came was unlike any I'd heard, and I lashed out at Darrian, marking his chest with my anger.

"Grace?" he asked, sounding worried. My vision blurred, and I felt like I was going to explode.

I didn't understand. I'd been so happy just a few moments ago, and now I wanted to fucking kill Darrian. Or fuck him. Yes, that was a much better idea. I wanted to fuck Darrian until he died. Yes, I settled on that.

"Darrian?"

I flipped around and pushed him onto his back.

"Oh, fuck. No, no, no, Grace. Oh, no. Fuck." Darrian jumped from the bed, highlighting the powerful lines of his masculinity. "This isn't supposed to happen. You're not ready. I'm not ready. Breathe deep or something; please, baby." He backed away from the bed, and my anger intensified.

I stalked toward him, stopping when the bed distracted me. It was a mess. A nasty, fucking mess. Growling lower, I stomped toward the closet, digging until I found the baskets of blankets he had placed there.

I snapped at Darrian, trying to get my claws into him as he bolted past. He dodged right, leaving me to destroy our bed. That's okay; I knew where he was. He wasn't going anywhere naked. He was mine. The smile that cracked my face wasn't a happy one.

Carefully, I remade the bed, stacking blankets and pillows into a much better pile than my previous one. This one even had an Alpha-shaped indentation. Then, I went in search of my Alpha.

I found him in the kitchen, shoving food into his face at a high rate of speed. Filled gallon jugs of water lined the counter, and my eyes snagged on them.

Grabbing one, I tipped it back and drained it. Glaring at him as I swallowed. He ate faster.

"Grace, I know you don't understand what's going on."

"Shut up, mate," I growled, not knowing where the words came from. It's like they came from a part of me I had never met before, and I was scared by that.

"Grace. Listen to me. You're in estrous. It's going to be okay. I'm going to take care of you, I promise. But you've got to give me a couple of minutes to get ready. We aren't ready." He talked with his mouth full. His eyes were worried, which caused the haze of anger to flee for a minute so that I could think.

"Darrian, oh my God. Darrian?" I cried out, dropping to my knees. I'd never felt such pain in my life, and I've known a lot of pain. It knifed through my core, bringing a scream to my lips and causing my body to seize up. Fluid pooled beneath me, and I curled into a ball, thinking something had ruptured and that I was bleeding to death.

"Okay. It's okay, baby." He scooped me up, grabbing as much water as he could carry. I writhed against him, screaming from the pain in my belly. I was dying. This wasn't estrous; this was death.

Then it ended.

Darrian had entered me, chasing the haze of pain away. I wrapped my arms and legs around him, thanking him as I rode his body in abandon. Each thrust, each gasp, took away a layer of pain until I could see straight.

I sank into him, going limp as Darrian took care of me, making everything better. When I came, fluids gushed between us in a flood I didn't know was possible.

Darrian cupped his hand under me. "Drink," he said, offering me his hands. Nodding up at him, I took what he gave. The cramps that were threatening to return when his hips stilled stopped. "Come here, Grace," he demanded. Pulling me on top of him so that I sat on his face.

I struggled to get away from him, and he gripped my thighs, pulling me to his mouth. His tongue found my clit, working it hard and fast. My back arched, and the next orgasm hit hard.

Like a man starving, he swallowed the fluid that poured from me, his moans unseemly. But orgasms aren't what I needed, not really. The pain hit again, arching my back and stealing my breath. Then it was gone.

Darrian had lain me down and entered me from the side as I cried out in agony. The snap of his hips chased it all away. I could breathe again, shifting so he could take me deeper.

His cock slipped behind my cervix, and I came instantly, gripping him to the point of pain. He let go, giving me his knot, and all traces of anger, confusion, and pain fled.

"I'm so sorry, Grace," Darrian said, tugging at my hair and purring as he lay behind me. "It's my fault; I should've been ready. I just never dreamed."

"It's okay," I answered. "I'm sorry about being mean to you," I sighed, scrubbing my face with my hands. "I've never done this before; I'm scared."

He smiled on my back. "This isn't mean, Grace; it's going to be okay. This is nature. We'll get through it."

The cramps hit again, and I threw back my head and howled. Darrian's knot slipped, and he fed me our combined fluids, easing some of the pain. Nothing had ever tasted so good.

Then he was inside me again, easing my pain and calming the frayed edges of my estrous. I couldn't believe Eve walled herself up in a cave and fought through it alone. The brief glimpses of pain were unbearable, and only Darrian could make it end.

He made me drink water, taking very little for himself. Sometimes I would come around and find myself swallowing cum straight from the source. I'd look up and find Darrian's head thrown back in pleasure as he rested his hands in my hair. Even then, he was caring for me. He was feeding me as he had always done.

I remember nothing of the worst of it, and only a little of the best. Darrian served, and as he served, I fell in love. Love isn't about pleasure or sex. Love isn't a beautiful body; those things fade.

Love is about service. Love is easing another's burden not only because you can but because you want to. Once we got into the rhythm of the thing, I never felt pain again. Darrian anticipated my moments of clarity and knew how long my body would rest before it needed him again.

He learned which growls meant what and what I meant by my angry swipes at him.

He learned when to offer water or when to be the only food I would allow myself to take. Everything I needed came from him; that's what I learned. I learned that, ready or not, he would care for me. No part of life did not include my Alpha; I learned that, too. And what a lesson. He set aside his needs for mine, and that is love.

Darrian was patient and kind; he ignored my anger and rage, and purred until his throat was raw. He loved me with everything he had, body, mind, and soul, while all I could do was take.

And when I roused again, he was over me, his face thinned from our lack of preparation. There were lines there I hadn't seen. Despite that, he served. I hadn't felt a cramp, a twinge, or a ripple of discomfort in days. I smiled at him as he plunged so deeply inside of me that I knew there would be a bruise. Wiggling my hips closer to him, I groaned, opening up to take more of him.

He smiled back; it was a little shaky and a lot weak, but it was beautiful. I reached my hand to his face, cupping his cheek. I could see clearly. My body, raw from the abuse it needed to survive, moved against his, not caring about the discomfort.

I pulled him to me, kissing his lips and tasting us on his tongue. His groan was my reward. As his hips snapped faster, building to the last knot of this estrous, I ducked my head and ripped the flesh from the top of his shoulder. I accepted him. How could I not?

I felt the missing piece of our bond snap into place, and in that moment, we were both made whole. I cried out, my voice hoarse. The orgasm that rippled through me was exhausted and gentle, but my body still demanded. It demanded what only its mate could give as Darrian shuddered above me. The hot flood of his cum bathed me one last time. His eyes closed in exhaustion and pleasure, and he brought his forehead to mine.

"It's over," I sighed. "Thank you, Darrian." Then I promptly fell asleep.

CHAPTER 18

DARRIAN

I'd been hit by a bus. Blindsided and unprepared, I entered my first estrous with my mate, hoping it wouldn't kill us. But here we were.

Grace lay snoring and sprawled underneath me, my knot still tying us together, and sleeping or not, we were both getting a bath when it abated.

Never again would I be unprepared. Her estrous had lasted four days, and my rut three. I'd lost myself right after she had and came back right before.

Every muscle in my body ached, and I knew I'd lost weight. But Grace hadn't, so I considered it a job well done as she'd had no weight to lose.

She wasn't pregnant. Instinctually, I knew that. She smelled perfect, but not pregnant. I was okay with that. Grace was doing well, and so was I, but we needed more time to fix each other. Babies are a lot of responsibility, and of course, I wanted them, but later, when Grace had healed both body and mind.

The bond between us sang a different song than the previous one. I could feel Grace everywhere. Her thoughts as she slept were peaceful, and her sense of happiness profound. Even destroyed, she was beautiful. She was easily the most incredible person I had ever seen.

The knot abated, leaving behind the discomfort of a hundred or more knots over the last four days. That was nothing compared to what Grace had felt. Her pain had struck the heart of me, and all I could think about was easing it.

Sliding from the bed, I tiptoed from the room. Using the ComLink in the kitchen, I let the few people aware of the situation know we had survived. In those few frantic seconds I'd fled from Grace, I'd sent messages to Nana and Jameson, asking them to stay away.

I found a lasagna in the fridge, letting me know Nana hadn't listened. I put it in the oven to reheat. Nana always kept a lasagna or two at the ready. Funerals, weddings, or the unexpected estrous was the perfect time for a lasagna. Everyone knows that.

Needing a sugar rush, I drank a gallon of sweet tea before returning to the bedroom. It was almost dark, and we hadn't slept more than an hour total in four, no, five days. I felt like a noodle.

While the lasagna heated, I took a shower because I was crusty in places I'd never known I could be. Grace slept soundly, her face relaxed and peaceful. I'd wake her when dinner was ready, but for now, I'd let her sleep.

I didn't know what it meant that she'd entered this estrous when she did. It could mean nothing, or it could mean everything. Maybe the suppressant had been ineffective because she'd never had an estrous, maybe not. Regardless, that her body allowed her to function properly for the first time spoke volumes.

I was humbled.

Grace humbled me on every level. She'd been tortured; I knew that. The extent of her torture didn't have to be clear for me to understand. Yet, she's thrived since coming to me. She'd never once looked back. Doing more than survive, she'd chosen to move forward. That was the heart of Grace.

Maybe I'd served her through her first estrous, but she'd saved my life in that courtyard in Greenville. In trying to save Grace, I'd saved myself. I knew that. My life had been on rails for a decade.

Sure, I had money and power. But what good are those things if you're chained to a life you hate? I owed Grace everything. I'd gone to the Capitol with all intentions of freeing her, but she'd been the one to set me free. How ironic is that?

I stood under the shower for a long time, enjoying the moment of silent clarity. I washed slowly, relishing every ache and pain I encountered as I went.

Nothing had ever been so meaningful. Sharing my mate's first estrous and learning how to serve her had been the most pivotal experience of my lifetime.

I was done. Gone. Grace owned me to the marrow of my bones.

I turned the water off, wrapped a towel around my waist, and ran a hot bath for her. She'd sleep better with clean skin on clean sheets, and she'd sleep longer with a belly full of Nana's lasagna.

I poured scented oil into the water, hoping it would soothe her raw skin, and when the bath was ready, I pulled Grace from her tangled nest.

She gave a hoarse growl at being disturbed but nestled deeply into my arms.

"Grace," I whispered, wanting to wake her gently. "I've got a hot bath for you and dinner in the oven. Let's eat, then we'll sleep all week, if you want."

Her growl changed pitch, going higher until it stopped suddenly as her eyes snapped open. "What's for dinner?" she asked, her voice slurred with exhaustion.

"Nana's lasagna," I answered, peeling a sticky sheet from her back and dropping it to the bed.

"You smell nice," she sighed, closing her eyes.

I couldn't help the smile that came to my lips. "You smell better," I answered, loving the smell of me all over her, even if it was getting a little ripe.

"I highly doubt that." She nuzzled her cheek against my chest, marking me anyway.

In the bathroom, I lowered her slowly into the water, her groan deep as the hot water surrounded her. "You're forgiven for waking me," she sighed, making my smile wider.

"Good," I said, using my hands to soak her hair. She purred quietly as I shampooed and conditioned her hair. While the conditioner soaked in, I washed her carefully.

Grace's pale skin was marred with bites, scratches, and abrasions undoubtedly caused by me. I didn't remember them, but there they were. None of them would leave permanent marks, and I was glad because she carried enough scars.

Before Grace, I'd never experienced a full-blown rut. That's something only an Omega can trigger. Male or female, an Omega causes the animalistic state needed to power through days without food or sleep.

I didn't remember all of it, but remembered enough. My marks looked natural on her body, just as hers looked perfect on mine.

"I would say I could wash myself, but I think that'd be a lie," she chuckled, laying her head back against the tub.

I shook my head, picking up her leg and soaping it to her thigh. "Leave the center bit, please. It'll soak enough for today. It feels swollen shut anyway." Her laugh was carefree, and I enjoyed seeing her sense of humor.

Grace had changed. I supposed we both had, but feeling her more clearly through the bond showed me just how much.

Her lips were curved, and her eyes closed. Her arms lay loose at the sides of the tub. I'd never seen or felt her to be more relaxed.

Leaning over, I rinsed her hair before rising to get a towel. "Upsie daisy," I said, pulling at her rubbery limbs. "Come on, love. I want to change the sheets before we pass out again."

With a sigh, she half rolled, half heaved herself and stepped into the towel. I dried her, tucked the towel around her chest, and left her to dress.

The bed was wrecked; I hated to ruin the beauty of it. But I stripped the sheets anyway, carrying them to the laundry and dumping them in the washer. I piled Grace's nesting material on the floor by color, then remade the bed with the softest sheets I could find.

The timer sounded in the kitchen, signaling hot food. After leaving a fresh basket of blankets for Grace, I went to make a plate.

She was settled on my lap, lazily eating her third piece of lasagna when the doorbell rang. I was so tired that I hadn't heard the elevator.

Grace whimpered when I set her on the chair I had abandoned. She'd come into the kitchen wearing a nightgown of the softest material known to man, no underwear, and no bra. She'd groaned uncomfortably with each movement, and merely sitting seemed painful, which, I suppose, it was.

My cock ached from overuse; I couldn't imagine what she felt like. There was no part of her body I hadn't used for both our pleasure.

Rising with a tired sigh, I went to the door, unable to imagine who would interrupt us. "It's Jameson and Lorelei," I told Grace after looking through the peephole.

"Jameson," I growled as I opened the door. "To what do we owe the pleasure so soon after recent events?" I asked, trying to seem more friendly than I felt.

Lorelei hid her smile behind her mouth and ducked past me to where Grace sat. My head did an unnaturally slow turn, following her progression. I liked Lorelei; I did. It might be too soon after Grace's estrous to accept anyone around her, though.

"Dude," Jameson interrupted my angry stare by clapping me on the back. "How's it hanging?" He laughed, moving to tickle me, and I almost went full Alpha male on him by slamming him to the ground.

Like he did to me when I met Lorelei.

And just like that, the spell was broken. Shaking my head, I sidestepped his big, dumb hands and pulled him into a hug, giving him the hardest noogie I could. The sharp breath he took was the only sign I'd surprised him.

"Bruh!"

"Don't Bruh me, little brother. What's up?" I asked, dragging him to the table and dropping him into a seat. "I'd offer you Nana's lasagna, but, nope." Laughing, I reached for the pan and dug in with a fork.

"You survived," he chuckled. "We wondered. We thought you might be too high falutin'."

"Really?" I asked, raising an eyebrow and forking another bite from the pan.

"I mean, yeah," he said without apology. I shook my head and smiled. Looking over, I caught Lorelei whispering to Grace, and Grace smiling through her responses. My heart eased at how relaxed she looked.

"Fuck you," I said with my mouth full.

"You seem to have lost your eloquence. That and about twenty pounds.

"I can still take you, asshole," I said.

"You could never take me," he answered, giving me a wink. "Things good?" he asked, casting his eyes Grace's way but careful not to look at her for too long.

"Things are perfect," I answered.

I hadn't put a shirt on after my shower, and the myriad bite marks, including Grace's claiming mark, were bared for them to see. I watched Jameson scan my chest and shoulders, apparently satisfied with what he saw.

"Cool, I'm happy for you. Mom is foaming at the mouth to hear from you. You'd better stay away; she already booked the damn minister for your wedding. That woman," he said, glancing over his shoulder to make sure he hadn't summoned her. Southern Mamas are something else.

The timbre of Grace and Lorelei's conversation changed as Lorelei probably explained what Jameson was talking about.

Call it old school, call it tradition, call it anything you like, but Southern Mamas don't tolerate their boys living in sin. Mated or not, there'd be a wedding. God may have abandoned us, but your mama wouldn't stop looking after your soul.

"Noted. I'll keep her at bay a bit longer," I said, glancing at Grace.

"So you think, Darrian. She's probably got an Atlanta minister on speed dial."

Lorelei threw a piece of bread at Jameson. "What, your marriage is so bad you're encouraging him to run?" she asked, her dark eyes narrowing.

"No, dove. Of course not," he said, giving me a quick wink as he dove to miss the next slice of bread aimed his way.

"Children," I admonished, finishing the pan of lasagna. I went to the freezer, rummaging for ice cream.

It felt nice having my family around. Meghan had never liked them. Oh, she'd invite Jameson because she wanted to fuck him. Because of that, he'd been forced to stay away.

"Hey," he whispered, slipping beside me. "I wanted you to see something before you left the condo. Lorelei insisted on being close in case something went wrong, so we're staying at a hotel down the block, but I'm glad we were here," he said, his voice low so as not to be overheard. He slipped a paper from his back pocket, handing it to me.

It was the front page of the local section of Atlanta's only newspaper, which also had one of the New South's largest circulations. On it were several pictures of Grace and me during our outing in the snow. There was a grainy close-up of Grace's neck as she twirled, her claiming mark exposed. The headline read, 'Who is the lucky woman who's claimed the New South's most wanted bachelor?' Over another picture, the headline read, 'The New South's Newest Princess; Who is She?' 'Ice King Thawed!' claimed the final headline, and I groaned inwardly.

There was a short article on the mystery woman along with a few eyewitness accounts from our dinner out. "He fed her from his lap, in the middle of the restaurant!" one witness exclaimed.

To make matters worse, there was an article on Meghan's death and our long connection. It suggested that Grace may be the reason for her murder, in more ways than one.

My hands shook with fury as I read. This would upset Grace, and it would upset our family. They had no right.

"Calm down, brother. Eve sent the paper a cease-and-desist order. We caught the guy who killed Meghan two days ago, and he's already been put to death. Store surveillance caught the whole thing. Turns out he was one of her many scorned lovers. It was never about the money," he finished.

I sighed, scrubbing my hands down my face. "Thanks. I mean, I knew my relationship with Grace would come out; I just assumed we had some time."

"You've been caught unprepared more than once lately," he laughed, chucking me on the arm.

"Fuck you."

"Fuck you, too."

"Thanks, Jameson," I said. "It would've been a horrible surprise to leave the condo and see this. Or, worse yet, find the press waiting." Clasping Jameson's shoulder, I pulled him into a hug. "Thanks for finding Meghan's killer too. It's a relief."

"You're welcome. That's why we came. The paper has printed a retraction on the story about Meghan but continues to speculate about Grace. Since you've been holed up, it's gotten worse. Eve hit them with a lawsuit on your behalf today." It was Jameson's turn to shake his head.

"She did what?" I started. "Never mind. Good. Maybe that will put them in check."

"Is everything okay, Darrian?" Grace asked from the table.

"Yeah, baby. Just catching up with Jameson and looking for dessert." We walked around the corner, and I handed Grace a pint of something chocolaty, taking the caramel for myself.

She cut her eyes at me with a raised brow, ignoring my lie. I'd talk to her later, but I didn't want to do it until she was well fed and rested.

I'd seen another side of Grace over the last few days, and I liked it. Our bond had given her confidence; completing it had given her more. There were no secrets between us now, and she seemed emboldened by it, and I was beyond proud.

I didn't want a wife who shot people from balconies with a bow, but I didn't want one terrified of her shadow either. It was like watching the cocoon fall away and the butterfly emerge.

"Thanks, brother," I said, bringing Jameson into a side hug. "I guess you *aren't* the worst thing to happen to me." I winked at Grace and punched him on the arm.

"Grace, you look amazing," Lorelei said, smiling brightly. "I'm so glad it worked out." Lorelei rose, coming to hug me before they left. I watched Grace's lip curl up into a snarl and felt her low growl before I heard it.

Stepping back, I pulled Grace to me, calming her. "Thanks for pushing her into it," I said, raising my eyebrow at Lorelei. Her grin exploded at the show of possessiveness.

"Right," she said. "Too soon." Her laugh was genuine as she hugged Grace instead, stunning the girl.

"Darrian's right," Grace said, her growl changing to a chuckle. "Thanks for pushing me into it. I owe you my life."

"You don't owe me anything. I'm glad it all worked out. Darrian, the warning still stands. Grace is our sister. Hurt her, and we'll kill you." Lorelei stepped back into Jameson, who wrapped her in his arms.

"We may be out of touch for a few days to a week," Jameson started. "Unlike you, big brother. We've plan ahead. If you need me and I don't answer, call Lukas. He's acting as little brother and chief neck snapper if you need him."

"Thanks, Jameson. We'll be fine. Uh, enjoy?" I added. What does one say for this occasion? I didn't think there were any 'have fun during her estrous cards,' but then again, maybe there were. Southerners had a card for everything.

"Don't forget about mom," he added, walking to the door.

"I'm avoiding her as long as possible," I laughed as we started the southern tradition of a long goodbye.

A mere hour later, they were gone, and Grace and I let out a sigh of relief. I loved my brother and his wife, but we were exhausted. Wrapped together, Grace and I fell into bed and were instantly asleep.

CHAPTER 19

GRACE

I awoke feeling better than I'd ever felt. My arms reached for Darrian, only to find an indent and not the Alpha that belonged in it. Then, I smelled coffee, and my stomach growled.

The clock on the night table read six, and I couldn't tell if it was morning or night. The sky through the open curtains was black, but that meant nothing. Distant city lights shimmered off fresh snow, catching and holding my attention.

I felt Darrian moving around with a light heart. He seemed better, too. Our completed bond felt natural, but it was weird to have so much information about my mate and his thoughts. I don't know what had gotten into me, but I'd known I needed to bite him. At the moment, it was all I could think about.

The things we did? Oh, my lands. I never dreamed half of that stuff existed, let alone could be pleasurable.

When Darrian told me we might do familiar things but that they would bear no resemblance to my past, he'd been right. Smart man, that one. I ran my hands over my body, noting that I couldn't feel my bones. I'd come to Darrian with most of them protruding, and even after days without food, I was still healthy.

This is what everyone meant by needing an Alpha's care, and I supposed they hadn't been wrong. The entire situation was strange to me, but it was far better than the one I'd come from.

I'd learn. Darrian hadn't done this either, so we would learn together.

Lorelei had joked about a wedding, and I wasn't sure what that meant, but I assumed it was how people became husbands and wives. I thought Darrian and had already done that, but apparently not. It was all so confusing, but I felt great, so I rolled with it. After a quick shower, I dressed and went to find my mate.

He stood bare-chested in the kitchen. His loose pants slung over his hips. He was far leaner than he had been, and I felt terrible about it. His dark hair was longer than usual and tousled on his head like a crown. He was stunning. Sun glinted off the sharp edges of his muscles as he leaned over the stove, stirring a pot.

I'd never seen him in disarray. Darrian was always immaculately dressed and beautifully put together. I'd barely even seen him out of a suit.

He caught my movement, and his face rose to watch me, his grin relaxed and easy. "Hey, beautiful," he said, dropping the spoon and catching me in his arms. He brought his chin to the top of my head, resting it there. "How do you feel?" he asked.

"Better than ever," I answered honestly. "How about you?" Tentatively, I wrapped my arms around his hips, nuzzling against his bare stomach. I remembered marking him with my scent hundreds of times over the last week.

"Same," he answered as he buried his nose in my hair and took a deep breath. "I love you, Grace. I'm so glad you came into my life," he sighed, leaning further into me.

"Same," I chuckled. Darrian pulled back, giving me an eye roll and a quick kiss on my head.

"You'll be throwing bread at me in a few months, I can see it," he groaned, dragging me to the table and pulling a chair out for me.

"Oh, you're letting me feed myself now?" I joked, not understanding where these ideas came from. "The bloom is off the rose, is it?"

"Never," he started. "I need to stir the grits, or they'll burn.

I watched as he went back to the stove. He stirred the pot before handing me a coffee with cream in it, not black like he drank it. I arched an eyebrow.

"Nana called. She said to make sure you had cream and sugar in your coffee. She'll be back tomorrow." He piled scrambled eggs, sausage, and grits onto a platter and set it in front of his chair. "Thank God, too. Just because I can cook doesn't mean I should. I'm no Jameson; you mated the wrong brother if you wanted a chef." He gave me a wink, sliding his chair back and inviting me onto his lap.

"I think I mated the right brother." I slid onto him and was rewarded by the low rumble of his purr.

"Mmmhm. You never had a choice."

"I didn't need one. Everyone else chose well."

Darrian fed me as he purred contentedly. When I was full, I leaned into his chest, listening to his heartbeat as he finished.

"Do you work today?" I asked sleepily, stifling a yawn.

He put his fork down with a sigh. "Not today, but I need to go in tomorrow. Today is Sunday, but before we go back to reality, there's something I need to tell you," he said, tugging at the tips of my hair to calm himself. Through our bond, I felt his annoyance.

"What?" I leaned back, watching him.

"The paper has gotten wind of you, and I'm afraid people will make a scene. It's supposed to be really nice today, and I wanted to take you out.

"Oh. Well, I don't really need to go out. We can stay here and open the doors on the terrace. Plus, there's the laundry."

"Yes, but at some point, you'll need to go out, and I want to be with you. The busybodies will get tired and move on, but they can be persistent. Let's walk to the store; maybe that will be enough."

By the time we left the condo, the sun was blazing, and it was warm enough to leave the coat at home. The snow melted on every surface, making sidewalks and roads wet and slushy. By tonight the beautiful white stuff would be gone, and I was sad about that. I liked the way it looked and how it muffled the sounds of the world around me. In the short time I'd been out of a cage, I'd learned that southern weather could be anything from hot to cold, rain to snow, and back to hot again in the same day.

Darrian rested his arm on my shoulder as we walked. Because of the height difference, it was hard to hold hands while standing. The sun felt good on my cheeks, and my long dress moved around my legs in the breeze.

We got some looks as we went; people would notice him and lean together to whisper. He walked on, unperturbed. At the store, we picked up a few items for dinner. I'd seen nothing like the thick salmon steaks he placed in the buggy, and I couldn't wait to find out what they tasted like.

We roamed the aisles, each picking up a few things we might need. Then I stopped suddenly, embarrassed by my actions. "Darrian, I whispered," looking at the cart. "Should I put that back? I didn't even check the price," I finished, looking worried as I bit my lip.

He laughed so loudly that the entire grocery store paused. "Oh, Grace," he said. "You can pick up anything you like. We don't have any worries financially. In fact, I need to make sure you have a CoinCard and emergency cash in your name. I'm glad you reminded me."

"I don't have a job, Darrian, and don't need a coin card; I don't even know how to use one. Nana made me use yours, but I can't remember the numbers for it," I stepped back from him.

"Baby," he said, his laughter stopped, and his face turned serious. "You don't need a job. I told you that you can work for me at the firm if you like, but we have plenty of money. More than we could ever spend.

"But Meghan took it?" I asked, my eyebrows dropping in confusion.

"She took a small percentage, love. There's plenty more. Now, here's the thing. You're my mate and will soon be my wife. What's mine is yours and what's yours is mine, Grace. That's how it works." He leaned to kiss me, and I stepped away, unsure.

"I don't have anything, Darrian."

"Nonsense. You have my entire world right here," he placed his hand over my heart, and I melted inside.

Oh. I supposed that was something. I smiled at him, noticing the strange looks for the first time. Other shoppers had stopped and were staring.

Darrian acted as if nothing had happened and continued to place things in our cart. After a while, I did too. Darrian handed me his CoinCard at the checkout, and after a heartbeat, I took it and used it per Nana's instructions.

He grabbed all our bags in his hands, and we walked into the Atlanta sun together. We were immediately accosted by a reporter, shoving a microphone in our faces.

"Mr. Battle, who is the young lady?" the slick female said, giving me a dismissive look. Her suit was polished, and her nails painted. Her makeup was beautifully done, and she looked far more impressive than I. My cheeks flamed with embarrassment.

"Ah, Natalie," he said, giving her a wide smile. "This is Grace, my Omega mate," he said, flashing his white teeth. "Don't get too close, or I'll bite." He half laughed, half growled at the woman as she tossed her hair back, making me wonder if he knew her.

"You mated one of the Seventh's Omegas?" she asked, stunned. Her quick glance at me was even more derisive the second time. "She's quite lovely," the woman lied.

"The most beautiful thing I've ever seen. Thank you." Darrian leaned over, kissing the top of my head. "And yes," he added. "I did."

"Aren't you lucky," she said, sounding like she thought anything but.

"The luckiest Alpha in the New South," he said.

"I don't remember seeing her picture," the woman said, causing me to remember.

They'd done some kind of article on the one hundred or so Omegas of The New South. I'd been under the bed, unable to remember to dress. Obviously, they'd left me out.

"She was always mine," he said, the tone of his voice changing in warning as the question got closer to the truth.

"I see," she said, looking at me again. I could see her confusion. Why would Darrian choose me from among the smart, vibrant, strong Omegas new to the area?

I wondered that myself.

"You've kept her a secret, then."

"Yes, well, I am an arrogant Alpha asshole who is also territorial and possessive, naturally," he joked, winking down at me. "I'd just taken a mate. Of course, I kept it from the public."

I knew what he was saying. Let the world judge him based on a stereotype the same way they would me. Darrian was none of those things, not really. I was nothing like the other Omegas from the Seventh either, but the world didn't need to know that, and I appreciated his efforts.

"How about you, Grace?" Natalie asked, turning to me. "How does it feel being the one to land The New South's most eligible bachelor?" she asked, smirking down at me. "Especially when many, many others have tried."

I tilted my head back and laughed as Darrian's growl grew louder. I could feel his distress through our bond, but I calmed him with a gentle pat on the chest. "Perhaps they didn't have what it takes," I started, using my smoothest voice. "You can't send an Alpha to do an Omega's job, Natalie," I finished, giving her my widest smile and a sly wink.

I looked up at Darrian and batted my eyelashes dramatically. He froze, his growl changing to a laugh.

"Indeed," he said, sweeping past her to continue our walk home. "Come on, my love, your ice cream is melting. Have a good day, Natalie," he said as we left the alpha reporter fuming.

"Well played," he said as we stepped onto the elevator. He shook his head at me, brandishing me with his most disarming smile. "None of what she said is true. Well, maybe some of it, but it's been a while."

"None of it matters anymore," I said, looking at my reflection in the mirror, wishing I could look as put together as Natalie.

CHAPTER 20

DARRIAN

"You're beautiful," I said. "I know what you're thinking, and you're mistaken. You're perfect. If you want makeup, wear it. But your beauty comes from a place Natalie doesn't have. Without all that, she's a troll. Your beauty is natural and comes like breathing. She has nothing on you, nothing at all." I leaned into her, my arms full of bags.

Yes, I had slept with Natalie before I met Meghan. I'd slept with a lot of women in Atlanta and had earned my reputation as a playboy.

Grace was hands down the most beautiful woman I'd ever seen. And it wasn't just outer beauty. Grace had a light inside of her that refused to be extinguished, and that made her more stunning. No one compared.

"Let me carry some of that," she said, looking at me in the mirrored walls.

"I've got it. You handled yourself well, Grace. It's the South. People are nosey, and they are always going to talk shit. Some of that will be to your face, and some of it not. Don't worry about any of it. Word will get out that I'm a possessive Alpha jerk and that you have a spine, which helps us both. Someday you'll spin the press like a wheel. I promise."

We walked into the condo, and I set the bags on the counter, moving to open all the terrace doors. Fresh winter air flowed in, bringing warmth with it. Grace moved about the kitchen, putting groceries away.

I lit the grill, watching as she pulled spices from the rack, deftly making a rub and putting it on the steaks. I could smell the spicy-sweet mix from behind her and knew it would be fantastic.

Grace had a way in the kitchen. Maybe she could have been a chef or a baker. My guess is she could have been anything. She still could, for that matter. I would never hold her back from something she wanted.

She chopped onions like a professional, adding in greens and a dash of vinegar. She'd taken a few quick lessons from my Nana and built on them. Grace was smart, funny, and quick on her feet. She adapted better than most and had her mettle tested early. Simply put, she amazed me.

I was in love. I laughed at myself as I stood near the door, watching the Atlanta skyline.

Taking Grace's steaks, I put them on the grill, watching people walk below. Some stopped, looking up. The Graydon was a historical building and one of the lone holdovers from a different time. One couple, in particular, watched tonight, staring at the building like eager tourists. Maybe they were.

I grilled the steaks rare, leaving them on for the shortest amount of time that was safe. Grace was eyeing them, and I couldn't wait to see her face when she bit into the salmon for the first time.

She needed to be listed as my wife on my financials and given access to everything. There was a lot to do now that we were bonded.

Protecting her went deeper than just threatening people. I needed to make sure she was taken care of if something happened to me. Later, I'd go to the office and handle the business end of our relationship, but for one last night, I'd just be her Alpha.

Dinner was scrumptious. Grace sagged on my lap at the first taste of the salmon, and I knew she was hooked. We ate light: salmon, salad, greens cooked with onions, and a small bread slice.

Despite sleeping all night, we were both still exhausted. That is the effect of estrous. We'd been awake for five days, four of which were spent in estrous, and one night wasn't enough to recover. As if on cue, Grace stifled a yawn.

"So, work tomorrow?" she asked, slumping against me as she drank her sixth glass of water.

"Yes, work tomorrow. Nana will be by, and you girls can get into whatever you want."

Grace's next yawn was obscene, so I left the dishes and carried her to bed. She was asleep when I placed her in her haphazard nest.

I moved about the room, going through my nightly routine before sinking next to her. With a sigh, she curled into me, tucking her head into my chest. I didn't deserve her, not really.

What manner of creature is used as a sex slave but still allowed herself to trust so openly? Grace was guileless and kind despite her past. I owed my ma a debt I could never repay. She'd been the one to convince me to take Grace.

I shuddered to think of her alone or with someone else. How much time did she have left when she'd come to me in the capitol's courtyard? How much? By the look of her skeletal frame that day, not much.

Grace's muted purr interrupted my thoughts, stopping my dark train of thought: the bond provides, I supposed. Even asleep, Grace calmed me. Tucking her dark hair behind her ear, I marveled at her and thought that maybe there was still a God.

CHAPTER 21

GRACE

For once, I awoke before Darrian. I almost gave a victorious shout, but I held it in. He was always up and perfect before I could stumble from the bed, and sometimes that perfection was annoying. I chuckled as I tiptoed from the room to start some coffee.

Nana had taught me to make breakfast, but I'd never had the chance. I took it now. When it was ready, I eased into our room, looking down at my mate. Goodness, that word.

How had I gotten here? How had I come to be at all? I suppose that is the more valid question, but in the end, the answer didn't matter. I was here, and I had a giant Alpha male to figure out. He hadn't come with a user manual, and I was doing the best I could.

The room was dimly lit by the rising sun, allowing me to see his features as he slept. Worry lines etched on his face, and I wondered if he was dreaming. I sifted through our bond, trying to figure out what creased his brow.

I brought my lips to his cheek in the barest brush. "Darling, wake up," I whispered, watching the worry lines fade to a smile. "Not that I want you to go, but you'll be late for work."

"Being the boss has perks," he said, reaching for me and pulling me to him. He tucked me into his arms like a child might a stuffie, sighing deeply into my hair.

"I made breakfast if you're hungry," I tried, feeling my smile widen at his behavior. It seemed Alphas really were just aged children.

"I smell coffee," he said, flipping me neatly under him and ignoring my surprised yelp. He nuzzled into my neck, kissing my jawline.

"It's all going to get cold," I chided him with my voice, even as my arms wrapped around his neck. I sought his lips and kissed him, thoroughly enjoying his taste.

"We have a microwave," he answered, leaning over as he undid the buttons on the dress I'd slept in.

I closed my eyes, breathing him in and feeling everything. His lips were everywhere: my neck, my bite mark, my nipples-his hot tongue found them all. I groaned, arching into him. My hands found his hair, gripping it firmly.

"Oh, Grace," he groaned. "I thought serving you through an estrous would ease this drive, but it hasn't. I need you," he said, feathering my lips with kisses.

He slid into my wet heat. No soreness remained from the four days my body had taken a pounding, which amazed me. He felt so good as he moved, and the feeling of our bond was overwhelming. We truly were one person. His eyes found mine, not letting go. The first orgasm rolled over me, forcing me to break his heated stare. He pinched my nipple lightly, drawing the orgasm deeper and making me cry out.

And when his thrusts became erratic, he slipped behind my cervix to hit that spot, and I came again. Crying out his name and clutching at his hair as if my soul depended on it.

Then he gave me his knot and filled me with his seed, making me cry out a second time. Despite being tethered to his body, my soul left anyway.

It came back, settling in, and I felt our hearts beat in sync. I'd gone a lifetime without this feeling, and I was never more grateful for that than now.

If I'd known such a thing existed, I would have broken in captivity. This was like waking from a nightmare and instantly forgetting it. The past was gone, and my memory faded. Maybe this is why I couldn't remember my childhood. I'd walled it away to survive being tortured. Now it didn't matter because I found a new life. I'd been reborn.

The knot held us together, and while I'd been thinking, Darrian had been telling me he loved me.

"Thank you for everything, Darrian," I said. I heard it ring true and caught the startled look on Darrian's face as he lifted himself enough for me to see it.

The look of joy on his face was immediate, and I knew I'd found happiness and not only peace. He nestled into me as we waited for the knot to abate. That dull pressure behind my pubic bone was a sensation I hadn't known existed until Darrian.

Until Darrian.

My life started the day I met him.

I sighed into his neck, rubbing my cheek along his jaw.

He sighed, too, long and steady, as he sank into me. The knot abated, and our sheets were once again soaked, giving me the feeling that this would be an endless cycle. "I don't want to get up," he complained.

"But the financial world needs you; I can spare you a few hours." I chuckled as his weight shifted and vanished.

I blinked up at the sight of his naked body, loving how the sun glanced off his dark skin. He held out his hand to me, and I took it, sliding to my feet and adding a mess to the floor. Thank goodness it wasn't carpet, I laughed to myself.

Who would've thought?

In the kitchen, we reheated breakfast and drank old coffee, and neither of us cared. Nana came, hugging us and congratulating us on our survival. She didn't even bother looking sheepish when she asked about my smoothie.

I blamed the smoothie for the estrous, but then the smoothie is likely how I survived, so I couldn't complain. Darrian left with kisses and hugs, leaving me for the first time in what felt like ages. I could still feel his heart beating in my chest and wasn't bothered overmuch by his absence.

Nana and I made small talk and cleaned up the lingering mess. We opened the terrace doors to let in another unseasonably warm day. She asked if I had questions, and I threw my head back laughing.

No, I had no questions; they'd been settled. Nana shook her head and helped fold the ignored clothes and wash the filthy nesting material. In no time, the condo was pristine again, and dinner was planned. I found that I didn't mind caring for Darrian and my home.

Eve and Lorelei had jobs and did them well. Darrian had offered me a job in his office, but caring for him when he couldn't was rewarding. He had a high-profile job that kept him busy. Would I go with him to the office and help there? Maybe, but I no longer felt the need to earn my groceries with a job outside of our home: Our home. For that's what it was.

In the afternoon, the doorbell rang, pausing my steps.

"I'll get it, Grace. Step back, dear," Nana added as I reached for the handle.

I did as she said, moving from the foyer and stepping behind her.

"Who is it?" she asked, trying to see through the peephole, but it was made for Alphas, not Omegas.

"It's Bradon and Joy Farmington; we're Grace's parents."

"Call Darrian. Now, Grace," Nana whispered, her tone leaving no room for discussion.

Startled, I did as she said.

"One moment, please. Mrs. Battle isn't decent." Nana answered. In one moment, Nana went from a sweet little old lady to a tigress. She shooed me away, miming for me to close the bedroom door.

Grabbing the ComLink, I did as she asked. There was only one problem: I wasn't sure how it worked. I'd been shown a lot of things, but using the ComLink wasn't one of them.

I thought back to how others had used it and pushed a few buttons. After trial and error, my fumbling fingers made something happen.

"Battle and Associates. How may I direct your call?"

"I need Darrian," I said, unsure how this went.

"I'm sorry, miss. Mr. Battle is in a meeting," she answered, only to give a startled yelp. I heard clattering on the line. My hands were shaking so that I almost dropped the Link.

"What is it, Grace?" Darrian growled, and I heard the startled intake of breath from whoever had answered the phone. "I can feel your distress."

"I'm fine," I started. "I think. There are people at the door. They say," I tried, my voice failing as I swallowed hard. "They say they are my parents." I felt my fear ratchet up and wondered how much of it was mine and how much Darrian's.

"Do not open the door," he shouted. "I'm on my way."

There was banging and slamming, then silence as I clung to the ComLink for dear life.

"Mrs. Battle?" A voice said through the speaker.

"Yes?" I stammered.

"I apologize; I didn't recognize the number on the link," she said, sounding worried. "It won't happen again."

"It's okay," I tried to make my voice steady because I didn't want to be thought of as Darrian's scared Omega, but at that moment, that's exactly what I was.

"Miss Helen," I said, reverting to formalities as I opened the bedroom door. "Don't," I trailed off. Let them in, I finished the thought in my head as the people in question were already seated on the couch, sipping sweet tea.

Again, I was reminded of what part of the country we lived in. The innocuous-looking couple sat, looking to where I had frozen in the hallway. The woman stood, opening her arms. I glanced at Nana, who gave an almost imperceptible shake of her head.

I stood behind Nana, unsure how to proceed. There was probably an etiquette manual for this very situation, but I'd yet to read it. I could barely read my name after all.

One would think that if a child was taught to read, they wouldn't forget, amnesia or no. It made me wonder about the care those parents provided. I didn't recognize these people. Yes, the woman had dark, salt-and-pepper hair, a color similar to mine. Her gray eyes watched me, imploring me to step forward, but they struck no chord in my memory.

I've been told my coloration is quite common in the area once known as the Appalachians, and I was hard-pressed to take her at her word.

The door slammed open, and wide-eyed, Darrian flew into the room, his eyes frantic until they found mine. He came to my side, gathering me into his arms. He must have run. His chest heaved, and sweat trickled through his shirt when I wrapped my arms around him. I could feel the glare he cast over my head, and his growl was not subtle.

"Are you okay?" he asked, pulling back and checking me over.

"I'm fine," I answered, looking up at him.

"Mr. Battle and his wife are newly mated," Nana said, stepping forward and reverting to formalities. She cast me a look. "Sir," she said, addressing Darrian directly. "This is Mr. and Mrs. Farmington; they claim to be Grace's parents."

Darrian straightened and reached his hand toward the older man. "Darrian Battle," he said. I could see Darrian's white-knuckled grip on his hand as they shook. "My housekeeper is correct. My apologies."

"No apology needed," Mr. Farmington said, regarding me with an expression I couldn't read.

The man was much taller than I, but not nearly as tall as Darrian. He didn't look like an Alpha in size or shape; he seemed more like a tall Beta. I knew little about dynamics, but I'd seen enough to tell them apart most of the time.

Darrian waved his arm toward the couch, looking at Nana over my shoulder. "Please take a seat."

Darrian went to the chair by the fireplace and sat without taking his eyes off the couple. He moved his arm to the side in a gesture I knew well. I climbed into his lap, tucking myself under his chin. He purred loudly, and I didn't know who he was trying to comfort: himself or me. Probably both.

"I understand your caution, Mr. Battle," Mr. Farmington said as he leaned forward. "We lost Grace a long time ago and have been looking for her for many years."

"How does one lose their daughter, Mr. Farmington?" Darrian asked, his voice low. It held the edge of a threat that was unlike him.

"Call me Joe," the other man said, reaching for his wife's hand. "Grace was playing in the yard, and Hope was distracted by a conversation with her friend. One moment was all it took, and Grace was gone."

"How old was she?" Darrian asked, his voice hard. "How old was Grace when this happened?"

"She was ten." The woman answered, looking at Grace. Her lashes were heavy with tears.

"How many years ago?" Darrian demanded.

"Eighteen," she said, choking back a sob.

Darrian leaned back, clutching me tighter. He scrubbed his face with his free hand, and I could feel his deep sigh.

I was twenty-eight. If these people were telling the truth, I was twenty-eight years old and had spent over half my life as a sex slave. I'd never stood a chance. Snuggling deeper under Darrian's chin, I refused to look at the couple.

"You realize I'm going to require proof that what you say is true." Darrian's voice contained a steel edge I had never heard, and it calmed me more than I could say.

He was an excellent mate; he would keep me safe.

"Grace, it's mommy," the woman cried, reaching for me as if she was unable to take it anymore. "It's mommy!" Her cries turned to sobs, and she turned to the comfort of her husband's arms. I sat staring, my eyes wide and frozen.

"Grace has no memory of her childhood," Darrian said. Rising with me cradled in his arms. "Now, if you'll excuse me, I need to see to my wife," he added. "I don't mean to be cruel, but she is my only priority. Miss Helen will make an appointment for you to return with proof of your claim." Darrian made no apology as he strode with me down the hall.

I heard the woman's shrill wail and covered my ears, and felt like I was falling. "No, no, no, no," I repeated.

And then I was back in that cell. The cries were mine, and a man was raping me. I let out a scream and tried to flee, only to be caught by my ankle and dragged back. My body wasn't even righted before he entered me again. I felt torn in half.

My thin arms were covered in bruises and grime. He pulled my head back by the hair. "Don't. Fucking. Run. From. Me, little girl," he said. Each word accentuated by a thrust of his hips.

I screamed as he pressed his full weight into my back with a fist. Something broke, and my breath came in gasps. He silenced me with a blow to my ribs and thrust once more before coming inside me with a deep groan.

"God, what a sweet fuck you are. So fucking tight. Fight me again, little bitch; I like it." He laughed as he used my back as a springboard to stand. He kicked me in the ribs before he locked the cell door, leaving me to gasp alone and in pain.

"Grace, baby. Come back, I've got you. I've got you," I heard a man's voice, and I fought him, too. Screaming, I lashed out with my legs and feet. I needed to get away; it was too much. This wasn't happening because I was done. It need to end, the pain had to end.

Digging my nails into my arms, I felt the relief that particular pain brought. I buried my hands in my hair and yanked at it, trying to pull it free.

When my arms were pinned to my sides, I fought harder, knowing I wouldn't win. Why did I fight now when I'd stopped fighting long ago? I knew how this ended; I should just lie there. It was better than the pain. Going silent, I closed my eyes, slipping into the blank space in my head that I had made for these moments. In that space, there was nothing. No pain, no sorrow, no fear: nothing. I went to that space, and I just let go.

CHAPTER 22

DARRIAN

What is worse than the woman you love screaming in terror and fighting an enemy you cannot see? The moment she stops.

Grace's terrified howls just ended. Her eyes went blank, and all the light that shone in her extinguished. She was simply gone. Her heart beat, and her chest rose and fell, but no soul animated her body. She'd gone limp against me. Horrified, I pulled away from her, and like a marionette with cut strings, she sagged in a crumpled heap on the bed, eyes open and staring.

Blood ran down the gouges in her arms, and a clump of black hair tangled in her fingers. She didn't blink, just stared at some unseen horror.

"Helen!" I shouted, not knowing if the Farmingtons were gone.

Wisely, Nana had kept her tie to me formal. When meeting strangers whose motives you don't understand, discretion is always best.

"Oh, my lands," she said from the door, her hand covering her mouth quickly.

"Call the doctor," I demanded, rushing to the bathroom for a warm cloth to wash Grace's face and arms. I didn't know what else to do, and the feeling of helplessness gutted me.

Our bond was silent, as if Grace wasn't on the other end. Nothing came from her side. My fear was deep and real. I washed her arms gently, not wanting to trigger another episode. I wasn't sure what had triggered the first one, but my broken heart couldn't take a second, and neither could hers.

This is what Lorelei and Eve had seen. This is why they thought Grace would be better off dead. She had calmed only after hurting herself and would require medical intervention.

And I thought I had fixed her.

I'd been a fool.

I picked her up, cradling her like a rag doll. Her body was unwieldy, arms hanging at awkward angles. I struggled to arrange them into some semblance of a natural pose.

"He'll be here in five minutes," Nana said. Tears ran down her face as she looked at Grace's lifeless body. "What did they do to her?" she asked, her voice cracking.

"I don't know, Nana." The words came out as a sob, and I knew I sounded like a scared little boy. And maybe I was. I was out of my depth and probably always had been.

"It'll be all right, Darrian," she tried, rubbing my head. "Grace is strong."

I shook my head. It wasn't Grace's fault, none of it. Grace's life had been nothing but torture and pain. I'd glossed it over, not wanting to know about it. Then a trigger I should have known existed was pulled, and now my mate lay limp in my arms, so far gone that our bond couldn't find her.

No, this was my fault. I thought I could help. I, with no experience in fixing anything but horses, had tried to fix Grace. It had been an experiment on my part, and I'd failed miserably.

Now Grace paid the price. Instead of sending her to the best counselors money could buy, I'd made her a DIY project. This would change. It would all change.

The doorbell rang, and Nana rushed to escort the doctor to Grace. I couldn't stop my growl and my efforts to keep his hands off her.

"Darrian," he said sternly. "Lay the girl down and let me look at her," he demanded.

I'd known Dr. Carver my entire life. He'd cared for me as a child, and he'd known my family forever. I trusted him with my life, but I still couldn't bring myself to let him touch her. "The girl needs help," he softened, and his hand on my shoulder cleared my mind.

I rose carefully, laying her down and fighting my instincts to protect her from the old Alpha doctor.

"What happened, son?" he asked, and I sat on the corner of the bed and told him everything.

When I was done, he looked Grace over, listening to her heart and lungs. Her vital signs were stable, and there was no medical reason for her fugue state, he told us. He couldn't say what triggered her behavior or how to keep it from happening again.

He agreed Grace needed to see a professional for her mental state, but warned that it may make things worse, not better, in the beginning. He glued the deepest gouges on her arms, cleaning the rest and warning that they would scar.

So many scars. Her mind and body were covered with them, and I ignored the warning they represented to her detriment.

He gave me firm instructions on caring for the wounds, but warned me there was nothing to do now but wait.

When he was gone, I sat at her side, staring. Dr. Carver had closed her eyes, but they continued to be unnaturally still. Grace's face held no expression; if I didn't know better, I'd say she was dead.

Nana sat in the corner, knitting from a bag of yarn. I'd told her she could go, and she politely refused, saying she would stay until Grace awoke.

Unable to do anything else, I dialed Jameson, only to remember that he was indisposed this week. I took his advice and called The Alpha. Usually, I would see to these matters myself, but my only concern was Grace.

"I need to know who they are, Lukas. No cost is too high; I'll pay for it. Get me all the information you can," I whispered into the phone. "I'm asking you as a brother," I finished, glancing at Grace.

"What's happened?" he asked, and I told him.

When I was done, I felt him pause. "Darrian," he started.

"No. Absolutely not, Lukas. Don't even say it; she was doing better. We'll get through this. She wants to live," I added, hoping it was true.

God, I hoped it was true.

I remembered her on the ledge, and my heart sank.

His deep sigh on the other end of the phone spoke volumes. "That you ask me as a brother and not as your leader is why I'm saying this. Grace may not make it, Darrian. You need to face that; it was foolish to claim the girl so soon. As a brother, now that you are bonded, you may not make it either.

"I will look into the Farmington couple. If there is anything on them, I will find it." The Alpha hung up, and I wished it had been Jameson I'd asked for help. The Alpha was a decent man, and Eve was teaching him the many shades of gray. But he mostly still saw things in black and white.

Eve was fierce, strong, and independent. She had. I stopped, remembering a little-known fact about her. She'd tied herself to a cave, willing to die during estrous rather than take an Alpha. Lukas had claimed her by force, and Eve had left him afterward.

She'd been held at the same compound as Grace for likely the same reasons. Though Eve had escaped after a short time, she wasn't unchanged, and she'd harmed herself too. If chaining oneself to a cave wall during estrous isn't suicidal, I didn't know what is.

Eve had gotten better, and Grace would, too.

Patience was a weapon, not a virtue. I'd been taught that my whole life and needed to remember it now.

Grace moaned, rolling over. I shot to her side, tugging at the ragged ends of her hair.

"What happened?" she asked, turning to me. "I feel like I've been in a bar fight."

"Have you ever been in a bar fight?" I asked, forcing myself to smile down at her.

"No, but I saw one in a movie and can only imagine," she groaned. "What happened?" she asked again, her face serious.

"You don't remember?" I asked, rubbing my fingers into her scalp,

"People came," she started, then her voice broke off. She looked at the bandages on her arms and closed her eyes. "I'm sorry, Darrian."

"Never, Grace. Never apologize to me for this. I'm the one who owes you an apology. I took your past too lightly. Sweeping it under the rug isn't helping either of us. Today proves that. I'm deeply sorry that I didn't try harder to help you."

"Darrian," she started, only to be interrupted.

"No, Grace. I'm at fault. You'll have the best money can buy, but you will have help." I pulled her to me, glad to feel her on the other end of our tether.

"I don't want that kind of help," she said, pulling away from me angrily.

"Grace, in this, I won't be budged. Sometimes, we don't know what we want," I said, lifting her bandaged arm for her to see. "We're going to work through this together, but we're going to work through it."

She shuddered against me, her shoulders heaving as she sobbed quietly. Nana placed a kiss upon my head and left me with my broken mate. Bless that woman for being a saint and dealing with both Grace and me.

I carried her to the kitchen and fed her from my fingers because I needed the connection. More than that, I needed to forget the impotent feeling seeing her lying there had caused.

We ate quietly, our bond hummed in peace, and other than the bandages, there was no outward sign that anything had happened.

When our bellies were full, she leaned back and looked up. "Are they my parents?" she asked, her face blank.

"I don't know, Grace. Do you want them to be?" I asked, rubbing a lazy circle on her back.

"I don't," she paused, looking thoughtful. "I don't know, and it doesn't matter. You're my family now. You, Nana, Eve,

Lorelei, and even my biggest Alpha brother, Lukas, are the only family I need. I can't help but blame them for what happened."

"Neither can I. We'll find out. We'll do DNA, check records, and verify paperwork, but in the end, it won't matter. The choice is yours. You aren't a child anymore, and if you want them to be nothing to you, then that is what they'll be."

She nodded her head, taking in everything I'd said. "I'm exhausted. Will you hold me? Just…nothing else?"

My heart broke for her, and I felt the sting of tears behind my eyes. "I won't touch you until you want me to, I swear." Grace's words told me something I hadn't known before. Grace remembered. Maybe she didn't remember everything, but she remembered enough.

I walked her to the bedroom, leaving her alone to get ready for bed. We lay for the longest time, each of us consumed with our thoughts. The hum of our bond was just a little off, for lack of a better word. The pitch wasn't quite right.

Eventually, Grace fell asleep, and I was left to stare into the night sky alone.

CHAPTER 23

GRACE

When I awoke, Darrian's arm was still slung over my hip. He'd slept with his back to the door, cradling me like he could protect me from the world if he only blocked it out. The sun was rising, and orange, pink, and yellow bands of sky made everything look different.

I hadn't had an incident like that since meeting Darrian, and I'd naively thought them behind me. My arms told a different tale. My scalp was sore from where I'd ripped out patches of hair.

I wonder if Darrian regretted trying to save me. Now that we were bonded, he'd doomed himself as well. I wasn't savable. There was no redemption to be found for Grace.

I'd expected anger when I awoke, but only found his worried relief. Darrian was special, and he deserved better than a broken woman. I thought to slip from him, and over the terrace wall, only his arm tightened to the point of discomfort.

"You will not, Grace. You need to understand that I won't allow it. We're in this together, for better or worse, and in sickness and in health. Together. I love all of you, even the jagged parts. I know it's not okay now, but it will be," he whispered in my ear. His words were fierce, and I knew he meant every word. By sheer will alone, Darrian would drag me through to the other side of this.

"I will do what it takes, even if you don't like it. And even if you come to hate me for it. You will live, and it will be worth it." I nodded silently at his demands, and he released his iron grip. Kissing the back of my head, he rose from the bed.

I stretched, lying a while longer in the warm spot he left.

"I want to trust you, Grace. Can I trust you?" he asked, casting a look at the terrace doors.

"I," I stopped, following Darrian's gaze because I could lie and tell him yes, but I didn't trust myself. I wanted to live, but sometimes those fleeting thoughts said otherwise. My eyes dropped as I shook my head.

"Use a complete sentence, my love," he said, waiting patiently.

"I don't think so," I whispered, the sound inaudible.

"Very good." And we were back to the beginning.

He didn't offer a long-suffering sigh or show any irritation at my backward slide. No, none at all. He went to a drawer and pulled out a key, locking the terrace doors. My heart pounded as he took away my only escape.

Darrian loved me. I could feel how much he cared through the bond. The condo was not a cage. I was having a few bad days in a long string of good, and that was what I focused on.

He left the room, presumably to lock the rest of the doors leading to the long, deadly fall beyond. Meanwhile, I dragged myself from the warmth of the bed and into the bathroom, where I let the water warm in the shower.

Unwrapping my bandages, I shook my head in dismay. I tried harder than usual this time. My arms were covered in long, deep score marks. Two of them had been closed with medical glue, and I wondered what poor doctor had been forced to tend to me.

I was a mess.

Darrian was right; this needed to stop. I'd never wanted professional help with my trauma, but it was obvious I needed it, so I would do as Darrian said. Two days ago, I'd been in the throes of bliss, and today I thought jumping from our gorgeous terrace was the answer. I had given little thought to the fact that it would kill him, too.

Maybe Darrian was strong enough to survive my fall, and maybe not. Regardless, my death would change him in horrible ways, but I hadn't worried about that. I'd given his life no thought.

Darrian had claimed me despite my problems. Somewhere in the shell of my soul, he saw value that I didn't. I had no right. It wasn't about just me anymore; it was about us, and I would try to heal in truth this time.

When face with having to wash myself for the first time in a while, I sagged in my seat. Possessive, controlling, hard-headed, and driven Alphas: can't live with 'em; can't live without 'em. I picked up bottles and went through the motions with a half smile on my face.

He was giving me space and could feel his struggle through the link we shared. Darrian tried to close the bond, but he sucked at it. He'd said he wouldn't touch me, and he meant it. It made me want him to touch me.

I wasn't simply a mess, I was certifiably crazy.

Dried and dressed, I covered my battered body in a long-sleeved dress that came to my calves.

"What do you want to do today?" he asked, passing me a cup of coffee as he plated our breakfast.

"If it's nice, I'd like to go for a walk," I said, hopping into his lap when he moved his arm aside for me.

Sometimes Darrian fed me with a fork. Others, like today, he used his fingers. The difference meant something to him, and since it didn't bother me, I chose not to ask. He'd made French toast, and he dipped it in a saucer of warmed syrup before offering it to me.

I ate in silence, wondering if he would ever let me sit across from him and feed myself, but as I couldn't seem to function normally, I doubted it.

When I was full, I tucked under his chin so he could eat and read the headlines from his ComLink.

"How does it work?" I asked, watching him push buttons and slide screens. "I just pushed buttons until something happened," I finished, looking at the thing.

He froze, glancing at me in surprise. Then he tilted his head, scrubbing his face with one hand before sliding back and lowering the thing for me to see.

"Grace, I'm so sorry. The ComLink is the first thing I should've shown you."

"It's not your fault I'm messed up," I said, glancing away from him.

"You are not messed up," he said firmly, wanting to believe it.

"We both know that's not true," I whispered.

He sighed, changing the subject to the ComLink. He ran through the details of using it and gave me the extra he kept in the kitchen. It was simple enough. His was more complicated and had more features, but they were intuitive once he explained them.

"We'll get one while we're out," he said when he was finished with his demonstration.

I nodded my head, thinking it likely I didn't need one.

"I've made an appointment with a doctor who specializes in treating sexual trauma, Grace. She'll see you first thing in the morning."

I cringed at the words he used, not that they were wrong. It was easier to ignore what had happened, and even easier to think that the past was in the past. But that isn't always true, is it?

I sighed, nodding my head silently.

"I love you," he said. "Nothing changes that; nothing could change it. But I can't look beyond something so devastating. We need to face it, and we'll do it together. We'll get through this," he finished, kissing me on the top of my head and depositing me on my feet.

After the dishes were cleaned and the kitchen tidied, he held out a long, black coat for me. I shrugged it onto my shoulders, and we stepped into the elevator. I still hated the metal cage, but it didn't scare me like it used to. That small thing gave me hope that someday my life would be normal.

At the bottom, we walked through the lobby and, hand in hand, stepped into the December sun.

CHAPTER 24

DARRIAN

The sun glinted off Grace's dark hair, making the black strands shine almost purple. She moved in a way she hadn't since the beginning, and her hesitation at the outside world was a blow to me.

She was so small that her arm bent at the elbow and up to her shoulder to hold my hand, but she didn't seem to mind. In fact, her hand gripped mine tightly as if she didn't want to let it go.

We did some light shopping. I dragged her into the ComLink store and forced her to pick one. Against her protests, I had it programmed and made her message Eve to prove she could use it.

We ate lunch at a small café, choosing to sit outside despite the chill. As people walked by, they stared. No doubt most of them had seen the article about us. She sat across from me, listening to stories about work and the stock market. I hated to bore her, but I had no idea what to say.

What could I say?

After lunch, we roamed the streets, sipping hot chocolate and window shopping. I could feel Grace's relief at being outside, thinking maybe she'd reverted to thinking of the condo as a cage. I couldn't be sure. Her thoughts were locked tight, which was incredible to me, as I couldn't keep mine to myself.

We moved to pass a storefront I knew well, then I backed a few steps and opened the door for her. She gave me a quizzical look but did as I asked, displaying yet another symptom of her larger disease. She had no will of her own, finding it easier to please me than argue.

"Mr. Battle. What a pleasant surprise," the girl from behind the counter said as we entered. Her eyes widened when she saw Grace, but she said nothing. I shook my head, urging her to remain silent as to our relationship.

Grace froze when she saw what lay in the softly lit glass cases. "What is this, Darrian?"

"This is a jewelry store, Grace. Diamonds may not be mined anymore, but they still exist," I said, smiling at her as her eyebrows scrunched together in adorable confusion. "Look around and maybe try something on."

"But why?" she asked, looking flustered.

I shook my head sadly. Grace had no clue why I would want her to pick out a diamond. God, Grace.

"We've been warned that despite being mated, my mother will insist upon a wedding, correct?" I asked, smiling again at the cute shake of her head. She might have understood the words Jameson said, but she damn sure didn't get it.

My mother was a force of nature that would not be denied. No doubt she'd already picked Grace's dress and was having it altered. The flowers and catering were indeed decided. The Battle family name was old, and my mother's southern pride older. She'd get what she wanted.

"Sure, I guess," she said, tilting her head to the side and looking up at me with scrunched brows.

"A wedding requires a promise from me to love you forever," I explained. Her hand flew to her neck, where my claiming mark lay. The white lines my teeth left behind shimmered like the very diamond I wanted Grace to choose. "It's an old tradition to present your intended with a diamond, my love. They are the symbol of eternal love, as nothing is stronger."

"I," she started, whirling from me and glancing at the counter. "But you already have that," she countered, making my heart burst with her words.

"And you have mine, but I insist you look at the rings. It's a trinket that would make me happy to see on your finger."

"I don't know, Darrian," she tried. "They look expensive."

Grace had no idea. Any diamond in this store would cost hundreds of thousands of dollars, if not more. There were no substandard stones here; they were all as perfect as nature could make them. I knew because the store was one of my investments. DB Jewelry was known for elite pieces. There was a lot of money in Atlanta, and I made sure this store catered to it. If Grace knew, she would shy away from looking.

"Just look and see what you like. And please like something big and gaudy. We can't have Jameson presenting Lorelei with a bigger diamond. It's unseemly." I hoped the joke would take the edge off the situation I'd placed her in, even though I meant every word.

She laughed, hitting me on the arm.

"It's not a competition," she laughed, her eyes brightening.

"I have seven brothers," I started. "It's absolutely a competition. And I must win."

"Fine," she sighed, her annoyed smile belying the pleased tone of her voice. I'd seen doubt creeping into the lines of her face. Maybe this would help chase it away.

She scanned the glass cases, her eyes quick to dismiss a piece. Grace had an eye for art and design. She picked the best works effortlessly, and that is no small skill. She had a knack for finding quality and could have been a buyer for Sotheby's with her skill had she been educated. It was heartbreaking to see such talent not cultivated.

She walked the cases twice, never asking to see a piece, and I watched her work. Someday, I would take her to an art gallery and let her loose. I knew that any painting she chose would be the best investment in the building.

She backed up, looking at something, then dismissed it and moved on. Finally, she stopped, turning to face the section of rings.

"This one," she said, pointing as she spoke with my clerk. "Though it may be glass, the stones are so clear," she laughed. "But in a way, glass would be perfect," she laughed, and I caught the hint of bitterness in it.

"You aren't fragile, Grace," I said, stepping next to her as the ring was set on a black velvet cloth.

"Aren't I?" she asked.

"You're the strongest person I know." I dropped a kiss on the top of her head before my eyes caught the ring she'd picked.

It was stunning. I couldn't remember buying it, but I must have. I thought I knew every piece in the store by heart, but I didn't recall this one. A five-carat pear-shaped diamond was set on a platinum band. A halo of smaller diamonds ringed the stone, but the band had no adornment. It was simple. It was elegant. And it was all Grace.

It was also nicer than Lorelei's, I chuckled inwardly.

"Grace, it's perfect," I said, nodding to the clerk. "Just like you."

"Darrian," she admonished, and I knew what was coming.

"You will marry me, Grace," I said, quirking a brow at her.

"Are you asking me or telling me?" she said, throwing her head back and laughing.

"I'm asking, but my mother will tell you. Pick your poison; the deed is as good as done." I grabbed the ring, dropping to one knee.

I'd pictured this moment a hundred times. At a restaurant by the river, or maybe on Stone Mountain, I'd planned to ask her to be mine. Even though she already was, this was important to me, so important that I dropped right there, presenting her with the ring she'd chosen.

"Grace, will you be mine?"

"I'm already yours, Darrian."

"You may be my mate, but you aren't required to be my wife. The difference may seem subtle, but to me, it's enormous. Maybe now isn't the time, and maybe you never want to marry me, but understand my mother will hound you to the ends of the earth until you agree. I'm trying to save you from that," I pleaded. I would use every trick, every lure, every advantage to make her even more mine.

"Of course, I'll marry you, whatever that means. I'm already yours," she said with a sigh, cupping my cheek with her hand.

"And I'm yours," I said, sliding the ring onto her finger, and it fit like it was made for her. Her finger was so tiny that I couldn't imagine it fitting, but it did. Perfectly.

We left the store hand in hand. There was a deep sense of relief in my heart. The ring on her finger displaced the sunlight, casting it in prisms on the sidewalk. The moment was perfect.

Yes, we had problems, but not with our relationship. We were fine, a little bruised, a little sore, but we were okay. Sometimes it's hard to be happy, but it's always hard to be sad. You have to choose your hard.

Patience is a weapon.

My ComLink sounded, and I stepped aside to answer it, watching Grace stare at her ring finger in awe. She wiggled her hand, making the light dance. It was adorable, and I knew I had done the right thing for once.

"Darrian Battle," I answered.

"It's Lukas," The Alpha said.

I took another step over, not wanting to upset Grace with what might follow. "Any news?" I asked, watching Grace play with her ring.

"They are her parents," he said without preamble. "We can get DNA, but the documentation proves it. Grace is twenty-eight and went missing at ten," he sighed, not dwelling on the implications.

I sighed, walking further away, not wanting to trigger Grace.

"Jameson might be my best hacker, but he isn't the only one," Lukas continued. "The Farmingtons are deeply in debt.

Communication between the male and another family member confirms they intended to use her connection with you to extort money.

I slumped, exhaling. "The mother, too?" I asked.

"There's no communication from the female with anyone. No emails, no messages, no phone calls. Whether she knows, I can't say. There are multiple interviews with her on the news after Grace's disappearance; she looks every bit the distraught mother. But I don't think I need to tell you that if he's looking for money now," he stopped, letting the statement hang.

"He could've been looking for money then," I said, turning my back to Grace so she couldn't see my face. I hunched my shoulders, knowing this was the worst possible scenario.

"That's what I'm thinking, Darrian. If you need me to step in, I will. What they are planning is a crime," he added.

"I appreciate it, Lukas, and will keep you posted. Thank you."

He laughed, "No thanks are necessary. I billed you for the hacker's time." He continued laughing as he hung up.

Jameson probably would've billed me too. Shaking my head, I turned to Grace. She'd stepped to a window further down the street and was looking at something as she waited for me.

It happened so fast.

Tires squealed, and Grace screamed as a van pulled alongside her on the sidewalk, making the hairs on my arms raise. She was snatched from the storefront, and the van tore away. It was over before I could blink, but the sound of Grace's screams echoed through the city streets. The van careened around a corner and was gone. I hadn't even moved.

I took a breath. Then I took another one. My fingers shook, and that shake traveled until my entire body tremored. Breaths came in angry gasps as gooseflesh prickled my arms, and cold sweat formed on my back. Hard and fast, expanding my chest to the point of pain, I breathed as I stared at the spot Grace had been standing.

I could call The Alpha. I could call Atlanta's security forces; I could do all of those things. Instead, something broke. Rage like I had never felt lit my veins like fire, eradicating everything in its path.

The careful mask I'd used to make me softer, gentler, cultured fell away, shattering like so many diamonds. This was my city, and Grace was my Omega. Mine. With each breath I took, I grew larger. It was like standing straight after being confined to a small space. Like being freed from a cage. My heart beat so hard that it hurt until suddenly the pain was gone, and I saw everything with clarity for the first time.

Jameson may have been raised like an Omega, but I'd acted like one.

My roar broke the glass of the store behind me, and my footfalls sounded like thunder as I pursued what was mine.

Through back city streets and alleys, over any obstacle that presented itself, I followed the beat of Grace's heart. I would find her, and they would pay.

CHAPTER 25

GRACE

"You're a pretty little thing all cleaned up. We should've let you dress up more." The man kneeled next to me, touching my hair and clothes. I dropped my eyes, saying nothing.

"That," he continued. "That look right there is why we're here. Do you know how hard it is to train that look into a woman?" he asked, laughing as he jerked my chin up to him.

"Takes years," the driver laughed. "And you gotta get'em young."

I froze, meeting the man's eyes before dropping them again. I knew him. He was a thing of nightmares to me. I remembered him. Everything he'd ever done to me played out in my mind, showing on my face. His smell, his expression, even his fingers grazing across my cheek felt as familiar as breathing.

"I could cum right now, watching you. I told you to run; I even told you I liked the fight. You'll see how much as soon as we're off the streets."

I was hunched in a dirty van filled with fast food bags, pizza boxes, and trash and knew if there was an empty surface, he would prove the truth of his words. I knew him.

I knew.

The van reeked of sweat, grease, and fetid breath. Clothes were crumpled into balls on the floor, and bottles of what looked like urine lined one side. Maps, pictures, and the front page of the paper were taped to the wall. My face smiled back at me. By the looks of the van, they'd been hunting me since my rescue. I was a fool to think they'd let me go. I felt the tremor start in my core and spread out as terror gripped me.

Terror was familiar and I couldn't believe I'd forgotten it. "I thought you were dead," I whispered up at him.

"Fuck, man. They taught her to talk," the driver growled, banging on the steering wheel in frustration. "That'll be hell to fix."

"Nah, it won't. Take me a day; two tops. It'll be fun to beat the city outta you." His fingers traced my jaw, grabbing it and jerking my face toward him. I didn't know his name; I'd never been told. But the way he looked at me? He would take joy in making me lose my speech.

"Bitch, we supplied those crazy zealots with whores; we didn't live there," he said, deigning to answer me. "The price for more whores was letting me use what I wanted. And I wanted you. I haven't had a decent fuck since that Alpha Asshole burned the place down and stole you. Good thing I was elsewhere that day."

"My parents?" I asked.

He backhanded me, whipping my head to the side and making me taste blood. "That's enough words, little girl," he said, scowling. "Not so little now, are you?" He grinned, licking his lips. "What the fuck your parents got to do with anything? Now, shut up; holes can't talk." He slapped me again, and the van lurched.

The driver shouted and jerked the wheel; the sharp movement flipped the van on its side. Metal screamed, and glass broke, sprinkling on me like rain. A roar shook the van, and the driver's side window shattered. I watched in horror as the driver disappeared, his feet kicking frantically. I heard bones crack, and his scream silenced abruptly.

Heavy footsteps echoed in the van, and the back door ripped off its hinges. It landed with a clatter far down the street. An arm reached in and grabbed the man's leg, jerking him out.

Something was attacking, and my terrified scream raised an octave. Blood sprayed into the van as the last man cried out, begging and pleading with his attacker. I crawled through the opening, thinking to run, but was blocked by a giant shadow and a hulking figure.

I was pulled roughly and cradled into a man's bare chest, my legs split around him. He smelled of fresh air, pine trees, and freedom. His purr was loud and deep, and his fingers tugged at my scalp. Without a word, Darrian carried me away, calmly stepping over the torn-apart body of my kidnapper.

My eyes widened in horror at the sight, but he tucked my head into his armpit and purred louder. Ignoring the screams from bystanders and the calls for him to stop, he carried me to The Graydon, petting my hair the entire time.

I didn't fight him, didn't struggle. This was my mate, and I was grateful. He was covered in the blood of my enemies, and his clothes were torn. How he found me, I didn't know, but I was safe. I was always safe with Darrian.

He kicked open the door to our condo, letting it slam closed behind him. Without pause, he carried me to the bathroom, turning on the shower. He still hadn't said a word.

He set me on my feet, purring as he looked me over. His purr changed to a low growl, and his eyebrows sank when he saw my battered face and bloodied lip. He lowered his face, licking it clean and rubbing his cheek against mine. I stilled, letting him have his way. He sniffed along my jawline and lips, licking my bite mark with his rough tongue.

Circling, he continued to sniff along my body, proving to himself that I had not been touched. I held still, understanding Darrian was gone on a primal level, replaced by an animal ruled by Alpha instincts. He ripped my dress, throwing it into the corner, and stepped into me. I understood. I did.

Leaning into the shower, he turned the water on, herding me in when the steam rose. He soaped my body as he stood under the fall of water, half-dressed. His eyes were alight with fire, and I'd never seen anything like it. He couldn't stand the lingering smell of grease and fear on my skin, so he washed it clean, nipping along my ears and jaw as he worked.

The hard length of his cock pressed against me, and I knew the promise Darrian made to me earlier was null and void. The thinking part of Darrian was gone, and the Alpha part needed me. He needed to prove I was his; words wouldn't work right now. He was past words and speeding down the road to action.

I wasn't afraid. Darrian had saved me from my worst nightmare. Again. Darrian wasn't a sex trafficker or a rapist. I knew what those things were now, and Darrian didn't compare. He was my mate, and right now, he needed something. That's all I had to know.

When he picked me up from the shower, forgetting to turn it off, and laid me on the mass of blankets that was our bed, I opened for him, inviting him in. I didn't need his growl to make me ready; I was soaked. His lips met mine as he sheathed himself inside me in one quick stroke.

I groaned as he moved in me; it was transcendent. I was stretched to the breaking point in the best possible way. And with him in me, I was made whole. We moved together in a rhythm as old as time, maybe older. I cried his name when he made me come the first time.

When I came the second time, praise for my Alpha fell from my lips. He was my Alpha, the best Alpha. His cock was magnificent and belonged only to me. He made me sing the song of the Omega, one I had never learned. That I had never known existed. There was only him. There would only ever be him.

He pulled away, ignoring my desperate cries as I begged to feel his knot. Hot streams of cum covered my chest and abdomen, and he purred as he rubbed it in. Yes, I was his. I was covered in the scent he made just for me, and it calmed us both. When he was satisfied that no spot was scentless, he caged me in his arms and fell blissfully asleep.

The shower ran. I couldn't rise and shut it off, and I didn't really want to. I was consumed by Darrian: the smell of him, the feel of him, and the heat of him. This was what it was like to belong to an Alpha. He'd always held this part of himself back. I knew that now.

This was not the face of the man on the cover of Atlanta Life Magazine. This was something else. Sighing, I snuggled deeper into the hollow of his arms. I didn't know where he ended and I began. Our bond hummed happily, and there was no discord between us. I tried moving closer, needing to crawl inside him the way he did me. He chuffed a laugh, tucking me into his armpit and resuming his sleep.

CHAPTER 26

DARRIAN

I awoke on top of Grace. In my sleep, I had covered her with my body. I reared back, thinking her small body smothered. The soft smile on her face reassured me, as did the rise and fall of her chest. She was naked, and I smelled my scent all over her.

I still wore the damp rags of my clothes and struggled to remember what had happened. After a shake of my head, it came rushing back. All of it. I groaned, palming my face in my hand. Poor Grace. Although I admitted, she didn't look unhappy.

As I went to rise, she snatched at me with baby claws, issuing a low growl, then she shivered, reaching for something to warm her. I tucked a dry blanket over her, smiling as she snuggled into it. I loved her so very much.

The shower was running, and it had probably been running all night. I turned it off, stripped my ruined clothes, and put on pajamas. We'd missed Grace's therapy appointment, and considering that I had killed two men on the busy streets of Atlanta and then fled like King Kong to The Graydon, it might not be a bad thing. I didn't regret a second of it. Faced with the same situation, I'd kill twenty men. A hundred.

None of it mattered because Grace was safe in our bed. They had injured her lip, but nothing else. Although that act alone was a crime deserving of punishment, the outcome could have been much graver. Grace was resilient, but everyone has limits. I hoped The Alpha agreed I was justified.

Loud banging at the door called me to the living room and away from my mate. Growling, I stomped down the gallery, causing the artwork to go askew.

The door to the foyer was splintered, and I found Lukas warily entering the room. "I didn't know you had it in you, brother," he said, shaking his hand at the damage.

My growl was the only answer I gave.

I watched as his arms went up in surrender. "Is Grace okay?" he asked, using the power of the strongest Alpha to calm me.

My growl stuttered out, and I scrubbed my hands over my face, trying to calm the instinct to throttle Lukas. He'd kill me. He may have stepped into my home, triggering my instincts, but he'd still kill me.

"She's okay," I sighed, moving to the kitchen to put on a pot of coffee. "A little banged up, but okay."

"You're not being charged with murder, Darrian. There are plenty of witnesses to what happened. Plus, it's on surveillance video. You've caused me to be up all night and to become mildly irritated, but you did nothing wrong. The law is on your side," The Alpha said.

I nodded my head, saying nothing. I stood with my back to him as I waited for the coffee to brew. When it was done, I handed him a cup and sat at the table, hoping it would help calm me down. My instincts were screaming in a way they hadn't since I was a teenager. My mind demanded I tear Lukas apart to protect my mate. It wasn't logical, but then few things about Alphas are.

"Who were those men?" I asked, hearing the strain in my voice. Every muscle in my body was wire-tight, and I wondered if Lukas could see me shaking.

"Calm yourself," he said, using the power he had to make the words sink in.

Little by little, my muscles relaxed. I took a deep breath, and then another, until I could see past the haze of rage that had settled over my mind. "Thank you," I said, meaning it.

"You're welcome, Darrian. You've been wound too tightly for years; this was bound to happen. Welcome to the dark side, friend," he said with a chuckle.

We sipped coffee in silence for a few minutes as my breathing evened out. When I was calm, Lukas answered, "Those men were known traffickers of black-market goods. It took some legwork, but we found they smuggled things into The New South from The Middle West and had been doing it for years."

"Grace?" I asked, shocked by what he said.

"Perhaps. The Farmingtons don't appear in the Seventh until around the time Grace was taken. They likely crossed the border illegally either right before or after."

"It doesn't matter," I said, looking at him over the brim of my cup.

"It does, and it doesn't, Darrian. The Middle West does things differently. Omegas are auctioned to the highest bidder during their first estrous and rutted a few feet from the auction block. It's their way. Maybe ours wasn't much better, but The New South is trying. The Middle West is not."

"Okay?" I said, stretching the word into a question.

"It's easy to extrapolate that Grace's father may have sold her. It would explain the fact that the mother has no communication with the outside world. If he bought his wife at an auction, selling his daughter wouldn't be a stretch. You need to watch yourselves where they are concerned. Their money troubles are widespread," Lukas paused, his eyes darting upward and widening.

I groaned inwardly, knowing what he saw. "Come here, Grace," I said.

"Is it true?" she asked, walking toward us.

Bruises had bloomed on her face overnight, taunting me with their myriad colors. Her split lip had swollen considerably, and one eye was heavier than the other. My heart rate catapulted as fury rolled through me like river currents.

I opened my arms, beckoning her into my lap. Lukas took in her appearance, his eyes narrowing into angry slits.

"You said she was fine," he growled, glaring at me.

"I am," she answered, crawling into my lap like she wanted to get inside of me. Sniffling, she tucked her face into the pit of my arm, kneading at me to purr for her.

The purr came on instinct. I needed; I took. Grace asked; I gave. God, the difference. The female spirit is the best of us.

"Grace, we don't know. We may never know," Lukas added, speaking gently. Despite his size and his power, Lukas had a way with the Omegas. Especially scared ones.

I felt her nod her head against my chest.

"Be more careful, Darrian. It took cleaners all night to pressure wash the blood away, and they may never find all the pieces of the one you tore apart. Not that I mind. I'm actually glad to see the façade of Darrian Battle crack. It's been a long time coming. I will say I'm looking forward to your brother's return. You're a bit high maintenance for my tastes." He chuckled, ruffling my hair as he moved to the foyer. "I'll make a call and have this door repaired."

"Thanks, Lukas. For everything," I added, watching him leave.

"Are you okay?" I asked, using my chin to urge Grace to pull away and face me.

She sighed, pulling herself from the warmth of my skin. "I don't want to see them," she said, meeting my eyes and dropping hers immediately.

"Look at me, Grace; raise your eyes," I said, reminding her of the rules I'd set forth so long ago. I'd take two steps forward and one step back every day for the rest of my life, as long as she was beside me.

"I don't want to see them," she said again, holding my gaze.

"And you won't." Picking her up, I settled her across my hips and went to make breakfast.

She clung to me so tightly, I could use both arms most of the time. Her head rested on my shoulder, nose buried in my neck. She'd breathe me in and sigh, making me wonder how I got so lucky.

After we ate, we lay in the bed, resting the day away. Repairmen came, and I heard pounding, sanding, and smelled paint, but I couldn't be bothered to get up. Grace needed to heal, and I needed Grace.

I made love to her again; I couldn't stop myself. My body in hers was the only thing that soothed the entirety of me. Her soft sighs and deep gasps told me she didn't mind. I worshipped her, glad that she was mine. She'd given me so much. I moved in her slowly, loving the gentleness of it. When I gave her my knot and she sang for me, I nearly cried.

Nothing had ever been sweeter.

We'd get through this.

The next morning, I dragged her to her first counseling appointment, for once ignoring her backward slide. She'd refused to meet my eyes or answer in complete sentences during breakfast, and I knew she was afraid of talking about her past. Of course, she was. Two steps forward, one step back.

That afternoon she was lighter, her smiles came more freely, and she laughed for the first time in days. She would see the counselor three times a week until the end of time if need be because there was help to be found there.

That night, when Grace slept, I got out of bed and went to the living room, pouring three fingers of sixty-year-old bourbon. Finally, I took my ComLink and dialed the number Mr. Farmington had slipped me when he begged to be in Grace's life.

"Forget you knew her," I said when he answered. "She's dead to you and has been for eighteen years. You had your chance to be in her life; you don't deserve another. She's mine," I said, the edge in my voice unmistakable.

"If you think I'm an easy mark, read the paper," I continued. "Go back to whatever hellhole you crawled out of and forget she was ever born. And if by some chance I find out that you sold your ten-year-old daughter, I'll kill you myself. Goodbye, Mr. Farmington." I hung up on him, feeling peace settle through me.

Grace was too kind. Maybe she'd give them a second chance, maybe not. I was not so forgiving. If either of them came near her again, I would end them. I cared not one bit who they had been; they were nothing now.

CHAPTER 27

GRACE

I awoke in a wash of bright light with Darrian snuggled to my side. How an Alpha so large could snuggle into an Omega so small blew my mind, but he managed. The sky was bright blue, and soft, fluffy clouds dotted the sky. I eased from the bed, tiptoeing across the warm, polished floors.

My face looked better. The swelling had gone down, and the bruises turned a pale green. I dotted powder under my eyes and around my cheeks to conceal them before getting dressed.

My hair had grown long enough that I could pull it back, so I did. Gyes looked at me, and for once, I saw what Darrian saw. I looked pretty. I didn't think I was stunning like Lorelei or exotic like Eve, but I was pretty enough.

I'd been going to the counselor for a week now and was starting to see the damage they'd done. The thing about damage is that if you can see it, you can fix it. It was a daunting task, but it didn't seem so hopeless anymore.

My parents hadn't come around again and was glad. I didn't want to see them. There were no memories of them. I'd heard what The Alpha said, and every word had struck home.

The what-ifs were too many and the situation too dire. What if my father had sold me? Even if he hadn't, which I didn't believe, what if he had? Sometimes there is so much water that the bridge can never be crossed. I hadn't missed them in the last eighteen years, and I wouldn't miss them in the next.

Darrian was my family. Eve and Lorelei were my family. The family you choose can be far better than the one you didn't, and I could live with that.

Speaking of family.

Today we were driving to Greenville to meet Earl and Annabelle Battle, Darrian's parents. I'd heard so much about Annabelle that I was already intimidated. Darrian laughed at my concern, telling me to 'saddle up, cowgirl.' I didn't know what that meant, but I was afraid all the same.

Something changed in Darrian when I was kidnapped. He'd always been so cultured and smooth. Now, he laughed and played, rolling around with Jameson or me like he was a puppy. I'd never seen him laugh so much or love so hard.

Our house was often a mess and his firm forgotten. We went hiking on Stone Mountain and skating in the park. Darrian was having so much fun. He hadn't worn a suit since that fateful day, and not one tie or jacket had been slung across the couch.

People came and went, and we spent time with friends I didn't know he had. We went out and had fun. Often his laugh was the loudest in the place, and he'd pull me into his lap, uncaring who saw. I'd never seen him fill a room before, and I loved it.

Something was freed when he saved me from those traffickers, and it was like meeting him for the first time. He'd tell some story, then reach over and ruffle my hair or pull me into a kiss. His friends would smile and get soft looks in their eyes, and it looked like they'd found something they thought long gone.

We climbed into a big truck I didn't know Darrian had. He ground it into gear, swearing he could drive it as I laughed at him. He swore I'd understand when we got there.

I watched through the windows as the scenery flew by. Almost two hours later, we pulled into a long, narrow drive, and I understood why the truck was necessary.

Deep ruts rattled the windows as we inched our way through the dense pine trees. The day was warm, so I cracked the window and smelled Darrian in the air around me. He smelled like this place; he didn't belong in the city. He belonged here.

Horses ran beside the truck as we pulled to a stop in front of the most beautiful house I'd ever seen. Graceful staircases led to wide porches, and it was like a dream.

A tiny, black-haired woman ran through the door and down the steps to meet us, her emerald green eyes sparkling in the sun.

"Darrian!" she shouted, swatting him with a spoon as soon as his feet touched the ground. "How dare you keep my daughter from me all this time? I declare," she said, beating him on his rump as he dodged her strikes.

I smiled as he laughed and howled with indignation at her swats.

"Get on out here," she said, looking at me. I looked over my shoulder to see who she was talking to, only to find no one there. "Come on, Grace," she said, holding Darrian's hand and waiting patiently.

He moved toward me, and she pulled him back, stilling him with her tiny hand. I slid over in the seat, dropping to the ground.

"Well, I declare," she said, her hand going to cover her mouth. "Look at you," she said, coming forward and hugging me tightly. "Aren't you pretty as a peach," she said, pulling away from me and holding me at arm's length. "Those eyes, Grace. You're stunning."

"Thank you, ma'am," I said, standing stiffly in her arms. I looked at my toes when she spoke until Darrian said my name softly in admonishment.

"Grace."

"Now, you leave her be, son," Annabelle said, practically dragging me into the house.

I looked over my shoulder at Darrian, scowling when I saw him laughing. He'd said his mother was a force of nature, and he wasn't wrong.

The interior of the house was no less stunning than the exterior. I watched it fly by as I was dragged up the stairs and into a pink room with more frills and ribbons than a Cotillion gown.

"This is your room, sugar. All yours. Darrian can stay in his old room until you're married, right and proper."

"Ma," Darrian said from the door. "Grace needs to stay with me," he answered, his tone worried.

"Fiddlesticks. She'll stay here until the wedding; you know the rules. Let me see your ring, honey. I know my boy is doing right by you." Annabelle grabbed my hand, flipping it over so she could see the diamond Darrian had given me.

"Oh, my lands. Darrian!" Annabelle said, with a sharp intake of breath. "I reckon that's the prettiest ring I've ever seen. When's the wedding?"

Darrian laughed, pulling me from his mother and into his arms. His hands found my hair, and he tugged at it, purring. I felt my shoulders ease and tension I didn't know I felt leave my body. "I don't know, Ma. You tell us," he chuckled, pulling me closer to him.

I peeked out at Annabelle and saw a deeply satisfied smile settle on her face. Her eyes were so full of love that it hurt to look at her.

"Well, I suppose we could have it tomorrow. T'wouldn't be nothing to put it together," she said, trying to hide her smile.

"Ma. Stop. I know you have the damn thing planned." Darrian stood straight, taking his head from the top of mine.

"Watch your mouth, boy," she said, glaring over my head at him. "Who ratted me out?"

"Jameson." Darrian was quick to throw his brother under the bus.

"Wait 'til I get my hands on him," she added, pulling me to her again. "Now, Grace. Let's make plans. The preacher will be here around one. The rest of the family will be here tonight."

"Yes, ma'am," I answered, quietly falling into step beside her.

"Call me ma'am again, and I'll take a spoon to you. You call me mom." Her southern accent was sweet and thick, and her words rolled through me.

I froze. I couldn't help it. My feet stuttered to a stop, and I felt panic rise in my throat. Why? Why now? There was no trigger here. My fingers ached to dig into my arms, and I trembled, but I took deep breaths like my therapist suggested.

"Grace?" Darrian asked, his arms going around me. His purr was soft, and the feel of it rumbling through my back calmed me.

One deep breath. Everything is okay.

Two deep breaths. I'm safe.

Three deep breaths. No one here is going to hurt me.

Four deep breaths. I'm alive. I survived; they didn't.

Five deep breaths. Name three things I can see and three things I can feel.

I smiled at Annabelle and moved my body forward. "Let's hear about this wedding," I laughed, smiling over my shoulder at Darrian as I left the safety of his arms.

CHAPTER 28

DARRIAN

Her eyes sparkled as she flipped her hair over her shoulder and walked away from me. God, she was so beautiful.

I'd felt her panic and the desire to hurt herself through our bond, but before I could act, she'd started breathing, calming herself. She'd never done that before, and I was beyond proud. She'd come so far. Did Grace have a way to go? Yes, she did. Two steps forward, one step back, but every day she got closer. We got closer.

My mother dragged her downstairs, and I took a minute to go find my dad. He was in the garage, working on an old car and sipping whiskey from a shot glass.

"She sure is pretty, son. You did good," he humphed, tossing a wrench onto the tool bench. "Your ma won't let me go near her, said she might be afraid of strange men. I understand. She'll come around."

"Now, ma doesn't know everything, but don't tell her I said that. Let me introduce you. Grace is doing better."

I dragged my dad into the house while he growled under his breath.

"Grace," I said, turning her attention from a magazine my mom was showing her. "This is Earl, my dad. He was working in the garage when we came in and wanted to meet you."

"Ma'am," my dad said, nodding his head to Grace.

At the same time, Grace said, "Sir."

We all laughed at that. Grace's default setting to feel safe was one-word answers or formalities. She may have learned the last one from me, but we were both learning. We were both doing better.

"Well, we might as well sit a spell and have lunch; the rest of the family will be here soon. Since you kept her from me all this time, I had to take matters into my own hands and jump at the opportunity to get all y'all together." My mom chuckled, putting the magazine down. It was a bridal magazine, and I had to laugh.

The thing was already planned; it isn't like Grace had a choice of dresses.

Lunch was fantastic, ma pulled out all the stops making her best dishes. She wanted Grace to feel at home and was smothering her with love, like it or not. Here comes Miss Annabelle Battle.

Grace smiled through lunch, subdued but happy. She listened to tales of my childhood antics. My mother took every opportunity to tell Grace what I had put her through. Grace took it all in, shaking her head and casting smiles my way.

She ate with a fork in her own seat, despite my wishes. If I'd pulled her into my lap and fed her, ma would have beaten me. That act was too intimate if we weren't married; I knew that. All her sons knew that.

Grace was hugged and welcomed into the family by each member. They trickled in throughout the evening, dragging girlfriends and spouses with them. They'd been warned to be careful of Grace, but as is often the case- they forgot.

And it was okay.

Grace would get panicked and then calm herself because she was amazing. Grace amazed me every day.

Lukas and Eve were the last to arrive; Eve's belly was so heavy that she waddled when she walked. It was cute, even though I'd never say it.

The girls hugged, and the smiles that lit both of their faces were one of the most honest things I'd ever seen.

"Thank you, Eve," Grace said, placing her forehead on Eve's.

"Sister," Eve said, and that one word meant everything to Grace. I could see it.

The bonfire started along with the cornhole game. Alcohol flowed, and the only reason Eve and Lorelei didn't kill something was that Eve was too pregnant to stand.

Lorelei had gotten pregnant during her estrous and was more radiant than I'd ever seen. She languished on Jameson's lap, and he purred for her continuously as she snoozed.

She'd said she hadn't wanted babies so soon, but nature had other ideas. I hoped the sisters weren't like my mother. Having a baby every year was hard on a woman, and I didn't want that for them.

Grace had options. Lukas might be too hardcore to use them, but I was not. If Grace never wanted a child, she wouldn't carry one. Birth control might be illegal, but that didn't mean I couldn't get it.

Grace hadn't had a choice in her Alpha, but she had a choice in this. If she never carried a baby, it was fine by me. Grace was enough. That choice was hers.

She sipped moonshine with my brothers and laughed with her sisters. The night was glorious. When ma and pa went to bed, I pulled Grace onto my lap, having missed her being there too long. She sighed, snuggling into my neck and breathing in my scent.

I caught my brothers watching and saw their soft smiles. They'd never seen me like this; I understood that. Maybe I'd saved Grace, or maybe she'd saved me. Maybe we'd saved each other.

No one mentioned Meghan.

As the clock at the bottom of the stairs struck two, I tried to pull Grace to my room, needing to feel her under me.

"No," she said, with a shake of her head. "Miss Annabelle says it's bad luck. You've already seen me after midnight, but on this, I won't budge." The gray eyes that met mine were new to me. There was a spark there I'd never seen.

My chest swelled with pride, and I almost cried.

"Okay, your loss," I quipped, dodging as she punched my arm. Picking her up, I swung her around, then hugged her to me. I'd never been happier to be rejected in my life.

Watching as Grace disappeared up the stairs, I smiled until it felt like my face was frozen that way.

CHAPTER 29

GRACE

I ate from a silver tray filled with eggs, bacon, biscuits and gravy, and sausage. It was the second meal I'd had where I'd used my own fork.

I didn't like it.

Lorelei curled my hair with a long, hot wand, and Eve dabbed gray shadow above the black liner she'd used to color my eyes. Miss Annabelle supervised with a smile, sipping coffee that I was pretty sure had whiskey in it.

My dress hung over the door, and what a dress it was. I'd filled out since coming to Darrian, growing curves where I'd had none. I'd tried it on earlier, hoping it would fit.

It was pure white with a fitted bodice. Thin, lace straps crossed my back and came over the shoulder, securing the deep, sweetheart neckline. My scars were exposed. All of them.

I'd panicked when I realized they would be bare for all to see, and then I remembered. Scars are a roadmap to where you've been, not where you're going. I survived. Not only would I not apologize, but I would also embrace it. My scars were part of me, and I was learning to love who I was.

The bottom of the dress flared out in delicate layers. It went to the floor but did not trail behind me. The veil, however, did. It was attached to the neck of the dress and flowed like wings

273

when I moved. My black hair and gray eyes were a stark contrast to the white, and even I had to admit I looked beautiful. I was beautiful.

Women doted on me, readying me to meet the man I was already mated to at the end of an aisle. Somehow, a single man saying words of prayer would make it acceptable for me to sleep with Darrian in the eyes of his mother.

And I was okay with that. I loved Darrian, but more importantly, I was in love with him. I would jump through whatever hoops were required to sit on his lap at dinner.

The Battle family took my breath. They were loud, loving, and overwhelming. It was an honor to be a part of something so vast that it seemed bigger than the blue sky outside the window.

Life was good, and it would continue to be as long as I wanted that. I chose to be happy. I smiled as they fluffed my hair and placed shoes on my feet, like I was a princess.

The dress came next, and every breath in the room stopped as it slipped into place.

"Well, I declare, Grace, if you're not just the most beautiful bride ever," Miss Annabelle said as she stood up and walked to me. "Darrian is a lucky man, but more than that, we are a lucky family."

Tears formed in my eyes as I said the only thing I could. "Thanks, mom."

Turns out the aisle was the stairs. When I arrived at the top, Darrian's eyes went wild and wide. I wondered if I was the only bride to meet their groom to the sounds of possessive, Alpha growling. I think it was everything he could do to keep from grabbing me and running.

His growl sounded through the entire ceremony, much to the chagrin of everyone present. Annabelle sighed, and Jameson shook his head, laughing. Lukas looked to the heavens as if asking why he had to suffer such fools.

I'll remember it always, for I'd never felt so loved.

Darrian had helped me find my wings, and I think, just maybe, I helped Darrian find his.

We said the words and placed rings on each other's fingers. We promised to love. To Honor. To Cherish. When I accepted Darrian's bite and gave him mine, we promised those things. On a primal level, this ceremony had already happened.

But to his family, it meant so much. When Darrian kissed me for the first time as his wife, I tasted his desire. His satisfaction was so deep that our bond thrummed with it.

He tried to pick me up and carry me away as soon as the preacher announced us. I was scooped into his arms and carried toward the stairs, but his mother stood in front of us with an angry scowl and her arms crossed over her chest.

Slowly, Darrian put me down. His sigh was so exaggerated that I felt it in my bones. He let out a short growl, only to be met with her hands slapping him.

"I know you didn't just growl at your mother," she said, giving a growl of her own.

"No, Ma'am," he said, ducking from her flying hands.

"That's what I thought. The caterers are ready," she said, glaring over her shoulder and warning him with the cut of her eyes.

He set me on my feet, looking sheepish before taking my hand and walking into the large kitchen to the cheers of the family.

"Grace, I apologize. You're stunning," he said, offering me a smile.

"Thank you, husband," I said, enjoying the deeper growl that word brought. I felt slick flow at the sound and stepped away from him hurriedly. "Let's eat."

His heated eyes followed me as I moved through the room, accepting hugs and congratulatory words as I went. I felt his need for me growing, and I'd never felt more wanted in my life.

We ate dinner and cut the cake. And as we laughed and toasted our new marriage, I felt Darrian reach his end. He backed me into a corner in the kitchen, growling and almost angry that I'd kept myself from him.

"Get in the truck, Grace," he said. "I need you at home. Now," he said, caging me with his arms and forcing me to meet his eyes. Only there was nowhere else I would rather be.

"Okay," I said, bringing my hand to his cheek and cupping it. He soothed, leaning against me.

"I'm sorry. I can't help it. You're so beautiful, and too many people are looking at you. I just can't right now," he admitted, his words honest and shy.

"Take the shuttle," Lukas strode into the kitchen with a smile on his face. "It's in the field by the barn. You won't make it if you drive." He clapped Darrian on the back, looking at me with a smile. "Grace, it gets better. If Eve hasn't told you already, it does get better. Marginally," he added with a laugh.

I nodded my head, not worried either way. I loved Darrian-all of him. Laughing as he scooped me up in a flurry of white tulle, he ran through the yard to the waiting transport.

"I'll make sure your truck gets home!" Lukas shouted, laughing so loud it vibrated in the air.

Darrian calmed as the transport's door closed. Now that we were alone, his instincts faded, and his rapid breaths slowed.

And Lukas had known this would happen. Champagne chilled on ice in a silver bucket on the bar, and roses of every shade of red decorated the counters. The cloying smell of them filled my nose, making me smile. It was beautiful.

Darrian shook his head, slowly whispering, "Asshole Alpha instincts," mostly to himself.

Laughing, I went to him, resting my head on his back as he poured us a glass of champagne. "I love all of you, Darrian," I said, echoing my thoughts.

He turned, crushing his lips to mine. His tongue slipped between my lips, and I tasted his passion.

"Grace," he groaned into my mouth, making me wonder if I'd ever said the words.

Had I never told Darrian that I loved him? Surely I had. He swallowed the words like a man starving, making me wonder. "I love you, Darrian," I said again, almost bringing him to his knees.

He picked me up, settling me on the counter. Furiously, he struggled with the layers of my gown until we were both laughing hysterically. Wedding gowns, a mother's chastity belt.

"Grace," he said, leaning his forehead into mine when he finally gave up trying to get through the dress. "Those words. God, I love you. So fucking much."

"I know, Darrian. I feel you here," I said, rubbing the center of my chest where our bond sang happily.

"And I feel you, too, Grace. You're so perfect."

I chuffed a laugh. "Now you're lying. You know I'm a sure thing, right?" I grinned up at him.

"I mean it, Grace," he said, his smile fading away to nothing. "You're perfect for me. Every nook and cranny of you is meant for me; I know that. I don't know why you had to suffer, but maybe it was the only way for us to be together. And I'm sorry, Grace. But if that's true, I can't regret your story." The serious look on his face caused me to falter.

"And neither can I." So overcome was I that all I could do was nod my head in acceptance.

The transport dipped, spinning in a slow circle, and I knew we were home. With a sigh of relief, Darrian grabbed the champagne and I the roses. Together, we walked the short flight of stairs from the roof to our door.

Yes, our door.

I squealed, slapping at his chest when Darrian picked me up, carrying me through.

"Tradition," is all he said.

Dropping me to my feet, he turned me, tracing the crisscrossed straps of the gown, trailing his fingers across my scarred back to my shoulders. He found a tie and pulled it. As the dress loosened, he unwound the straps, baring my back to him.

He traced the lines of the scars to where the gown had puddled at my waist. His dexterous fingers found the hooks, unlatching them from the eye, and the gown pooled at my feet.

Slowly, he turned me to face him, his fingers touching the only scar he'd given me.

"There is no woman more beautiful, Grace," he said, skimming his fingers across my taut nipples.

"Thank you," I answered, swallowing the denial and accepting what he felt to be true.

I stood before him, naked except for the white stockings and garters that held them. His family had assured me, as I slipped my panties off under my dress, that this was also tradition. And despite my misgivings, when his breath hitched, I knew they'd been right.

"Grace," he said, his eyes roaming my body.

The look of appreciation fueled me, and I reached out to him, undoing the buttons of his white shirt one by one before slipping his jacket and shirt off his arms.

Now it was my turn to hum appreciatively. Darrian in tuxedo pants, stripped to the waist, should be a tradition. He should wear this look every day. I'd seen nothing so perfect as his tan skin over hard muscle dancing under my palms.

My hand traced downward, and I cupped his erection, tipping my head back with a groan. And that was the end of that.

I was hauled off my feet, down the gallery, and into our room before I could protest. My hands were everywhere, touching every part of Darrian that I could reach. Our lips crashed together in mutual need as fire raced across my skin so hot that it was painful.

It was frantic. I laugh about it now. We were like two teens unable to temper our needs. His pants were down, and he was in me before my back hit the bed. I bucked into him, needing him more than I ever had. Who knew a wedding ring could be so sexy?

Our lips fought for the next kiss, and our hands roamed as he slid into me. He hit that secret spot, and I wailed an orgasm so brutal that it took my breath and made me see stars. And still, Darrian worshipped me.

He praised every attribute I had, his words filled with love and desire. I came again, this one rolling over me like the ocean: powerful and smooth, but no less destructive. I felt my body clenching him so tightly that he shuddered.

"Grace, I can't." One more thrust and he cried out, dropping his body around me when his knot flared.

Forehead to forehead, we struggled to catch our breath.

"That was incredible. You're incredible." Two hearts beat in time within my chest, and I smiled at him. Brushing the hair from his eyes, I agreed with him.

"You make me feel perfect."

"You are perfect," he said, nestling his head into the crook of my neck.

Almost like it knew our desire to be joined, the knot held us for a long time. When it abated, Darrian immediately started making love to me again.

This time, he went slowly, his long, powerful strokes sending me over the edge more times than I could count, drawing my song from me. When I was limp under him, my lips raw from his kisses, and my body spent of orgasms, he came again, filling me with hot streams which the knot held in place.

I had wanted to taste him the second time, but I'd been too bliss-blown to say the words or move my limbs.

Tomorrow.

I will taste him tomorrow.

Epilogue

Darrian

Grace holds Emmie on her lap, laughing at the baby's antics. The little red-haired, Omega spitfire that looks just like her mother throws her head back, laughing in the way only the innocent can.

I feel bad for Lukas. Almost. He has two red-haired Omegas to protect, and by the looks of the littlest one, it won't be easy. She'll have a weapon in her hand before she can walk.

Grace is smiling into the baby's face, making my heart melt. She's come such a long way. Six months of intense therapy have changed her. I think maybe she's coming to see herself as I do and accept her past for what it is.

A month ago, I unlocked the balcony doors and let the spring air into our home for the first time. Grace went immediately to the terrace, forcing me to trust her as I watched in fear.

Instead of jumping to her death, she curled up in a chair and read the young-adult book she was so proud of. During my absences, she'd thrown herself into her studies, learning everything she could. I'd hired Grace a Beta tutor, and the woman said that Grace was the quickest study she'd ever met.

I believe it. Grace approached everything with, well, grace. Resilient, kind, and forgiving, Grace was the epitome of life, survival, and adaptation to me. I'd been lost to her the second she stepped onto the stones in that courtyard. Her gray eyes resigned; she had surrendered in more ways than one, but in the end, she'd won. She'd won more than my heart; she'd won everything.

Earlier, I'd taken her to that art gallery, not blinking when she suggested I buy a painting from an up-and-coming artist. Grace has a knack. Someday, it would make us a fortune. She'd looked at home, sipping champagne with Atlanta's elite as she carried on fluent conversations with them.

Was every day perfect? No, it was not. Two steps forward, one step back, but we were always moving in the right direction.

Grace had an implantable birth control device placed in her arm. It gave her a few years to heal and decide what she wanted. Money could buy almost anything, legal or not. I would never force a child on her if she didn't want one.

Until me, and maybe after, her life had been nothing but pain, and I refused to give in to the desire to see her body round with my child. Maybe someday, maybe never, and either way was fine by me.

Another estrous came and went, and it had been glorious. We'd been ready, I thought with a smile. Not like the first time. Coming through the other side with her had left me calmer. Oh,

I still needed Grace. Daily. But the broken pieces of my Alpha instincts had come together, leaving me less unpredictable and more like myself.

"What do you think?" Lukas asked, dragging my attention from my wife and his daughter.

"About what, Sir?" I asked on reflex.

"About what I just said," he chuckled, leaning back into Eve.

Eve sat next to him on the couch, watching Grace and Emmie play. The soft smile on her face telling. Oh, motherhood hadn't softened Eve, not in the least, but it had tempered the quickness of her bite just a little.

"Um?" I tried, looking frantically at Grace, as if she might have the answer, but she was in another world. A world where there was only her and Emmie.

"I said," Lukas paused, glaring at me. "That I had the oddest request last week. I wanted your opinion," he adds, glancing at Eve from the corner of his eye.

Oh no. Whatever it was, she wasn't going to like it. He'd likely brought her here to mitigate the damage. She wouldn't destroy my house like she might her own. She also wouldn't physically fight her Alpha in the presence of others. Too much anyway.

"Do tell?" I ask, straightening as I wait for the one-two punch.

"The Galluh fighters have asked to be allowed to court an Omega," The Alpha said off-handedly.

"I mean, okay?" I said, not sure what the issue was.

"One Omega," he amended, watching Eve's reaction from the corner of his eyes. "They do everything together, and they think having two Omegas would split their focus. They're my best hunters, and I don't want to screw that up," he added. "I trust what they say; they are uncannily united." He sighed, shifting his weight.

"It's not uncommon," Eve said, turning her bright blue eyes to Lukas.

"It's not allowed," The Alpha said with a growl.

Eve tipped her head back and laughed, her red hair cascading down her back.

"Do not laugh at me," Lukas threatened.

"Why ever not?" Eve said, patting his arm. "You're hysterical. Regardless, it is not an uncommon practice. Many women in the Seventh have more than one mate. Life can be hard, and more hands make for lighter work," she added. "I don't see the problem. If they are your best hunters, why rock the boat?" she asked.

"Because it's not allowed," Lukas answered.

"Then why are you asking about it, Luke?" she asked, her eyes knowing.

When Eve and Lukas met, he saw the world in black and white. Eve had taught him about all the grays and the reds. He is learning, but it is still a struggle for him.

"You say they're hunters?" Eve asked, the wheels in her mind turning.

"Yes, of all species," he added, causing her brow to arch at his answer.

I knew the Galluh men. Bala and Jah hunted animals for the food banks, but they also hunted men. They were the finest assassins and sharpshooters The New South employed. The men came from a remote place buried by time and the war. Not having access to their island, they now lived as close to the sea as they could. Jameson talked about them endlessly. They were different from the other Marines, and the difference made for great stories.

"Hmm," Eve said thoughtfully. "I think I know just the Omega. She comes from an area of West Virginia heavily populated with Polygamous relationships. It would not be unexpected of her.

"Eve, I said that it is not allowed," The Alpha bellowed, amusing Emmie, who crawled to his legs, pulled herself to stand, and looked at him.

The look was priceless. It was also the same look of incredulity that Eve wore. Poor, poor, Lukas.

"And I have said, why rock the boat, dear?" she said, patting his arm and kissing his cheek. "Her name is Tosha, but she goes by Tosh. I'll see if she is amenable."

I shook my head, smiling as I looked away. Grace watched the interaction with rapt attention, dropping her eyes to Emmie when I caught her watching. I could see the confusion on her face and knew we would talk about this later.

The Alpha and Eve left not long after; he fuming, and she triumphant. Their relationship would always be a war neither would win, but both would enjoy fighting. It's just how they were. There was no surrender in either of them.

In their absence, our house was quiet. And in the silence, I heard Grace whisper, "I think I may want one." Her voice was barely audible.

"Another mate, my love?" I asked, hoping that's not what she meant, but knowing I'd give her anything she asked for.

"No. A baby," she said, and my heart stilled. "Not yet, but not no," she said, her voice cracking with emotion.

"The choice is yours, Grace. Always and forever yours." I leaned my forehead against hers, loving the way she smelled.

"And for that and so much more," she said. "I love you."

My need for her was too great, and I scooped her up, carrying her to our room, where her lips promptly found my cock. It was her new favorite thing, and I'll never understand why.

This was the one thing we fought over. I wanted to be inside of her and watch her shatter beneath me, but she wanted to drink me down, and oh, it was hard not to want the same thing. No pun intended.

Grace bobbed, bringing me to my knees. She followed me down until I was on my back and at her mercy. Maybe this time I would let her win.

Her hand found my knot, and she worked me expertly. She'd learned just how to make me cum in short order, and there was nothing I could do to fight her on it or hold back. She controlled; I surrendered.

Within minutes, she gripped my knot so it wouldn't expand and drank everything I offered. Almost frantically, she squeezed me until the last drop was gone, her groans of appreciation making my balls sizzle. Maybe those smoothies hadn't been the best idea, after all. Grace seemed to need what she took, and I would not begrudge her anything.

With a soft moan, she flopped to my side, pupils bliss-blown and unfocused. Only she started something we would never finish. As long as we lived, this need between us would never be finished.

I slipped between her legs, loving the groan as she tried to rally her cum drunk body for me. This time, I controlled, and she surrendered. She in the Omega way, and my purr made her open every part of herself to me: her heart, her body, her mind, and her grace. They were mine.

Grace was all mine.

DEAR READER,

I absolutely loved Darrian in The Omega Challenge, and I'm still crazy about him in An Alpha's Grace. And Grace? She's an angel. No, really. She reminds me of someone I know and makes me love her more for it.

What's next? I've been working on a project for a few years that is near and dear to my heart. I've never been in the right headspace to finish it, but have been building toward it. I'm there now, and I can't wait to share it when it's done.

Don't worry, The Omegas of the New South will be back soon. Oh, and...guess who is talking again and wants to be heard? No, really. Guess. I'm not telling.

Ever yours,

Sharilyn

Widowmaker

Gravedigger

Queenmaker- coming Summer 2026

Follow Sharilyn on Facebook, Instagram, Goodreads, and her plain old website.

www.sharilynskye.com

About Sharilyn:

Sharilyn spent most of her early years on the Grand Strand of SC, annoying local police officers and pretty much everyone else with her fast cars and loud music. She graduated from the University of South Carolina and now lives on a small farm outside Morgantown, West Virginia, with her family and a menagerie of cats, horses, and visiting wildlife.

Sharilyn writes urban fantasy, fairy tales, Omegaverse romance, and women's fiction. Each title in her Omegaverse series, Omegas of The New South, spent weeks on Amazon's best-sellers list. An Omega's Dance and An Alpha's Price were USA Today and Amazon Best Sellers, and her Healer series has a following that borders on cultish. (She adores you, you crazy Lara Hennessey fans!)

She loves showing Quarter Horses, trail riding, reading, drinking coffee, driving her vintage Corvette, and being annoyed by her kids. If she's missing, check the garage or look for the horse trailer. If one is missing, no worries; she'll be back. Probably.   www.sharilynskye.com

www.ingramcontent.com/pod-product-compliance
Lightning Source LLC
Chambersburg PA
CBHW070849260626
47170CB00007B/2553